U0085546

超強英語力！

全真模擬＋精闢解析

修訂四版

聽說＋讀寫

全民英檢初級模擬試題

附 解析本
電子朗讀音檔

Barbara Kuo　編著

三民書局

作者序

在 YouTube 上觀看 Tesla 創辦人 Elon Musk 的預測，包含全自動駕駛車的成熟、衛星網路的問世、大腦可植入晶片以幫助治癒腦部相關疾病、太陽能成為綠能主流，才驚覺到我愛看的科幻片場景已經出現在真實人生。

疫情期間參加了一場 NPDL 全球夥伴會議， 會議中有來自十個國家約 500 人的線上會議，其中有兩次的隨機分組會議各別進行 20 分鐘討論分享，臺灣也有多所學校的老師參與。 我發現其他國家的老師， 多數為英語系國家，且都侃侃而談，相對地，臺灣的老師鮮少發言。此時的我當然要挺身而出，至少發言 2～3 分鐘，分享臺灣在疫情下的教育環境。

科技的發展以及防疫的成功，這兩件看似很平常的生活小事，我真心覺得臺灣做得很棒。但是在需要緊密的溝通與合作的全球化時代，擁有全球移動力的最關鍵籌碼就是語言能力的培養。擁有良好的語言能力，不僅能提前接觸到新資訊，也能擁有更多表達機會。談到語言力，想當然的就是從小培養，日日不間斷。那麼如何檢測自己的英語力？我想最直接的方法就是設定目標，參加英語檢定。

撰寫這本書主要目的是要和大家分享如何練習，並將學習的成效轉化在檢定的成績上。同時也期待每位讀者都能獲得實際的學習成果，確實提升英語實力。

Barbara Kuo

全民英檢初級簡介

　　新制全民英檢測驗是為了因應教育部 108 課綱以「核心素養」精神為主軸,在測驗題型上做了一些調整,以符合現代人對英文的需求,內容更貼近日常生活,且納入更多元的圖表題、圖片選擇題、多文本題型等,達到整合資訊及活用英文的能力。因此本書經分析財團法人語言訓練測驗中心所公告之內容,特別編製符合 2021 年官方最新題型的《全民英檢初級模擬試題(修訂四版)》,讓考生熟悉最新題型,做全方位的準備。

一、檢測程度

　　初級具有基礎英語能力,能理解和使用淺易日常用語。

二、檢測對象

　　一般社會人士及各級學校學生。

三、測驗項目新舊制對照

　　聽力測驗的題型和題數不變,第四部分:「短文聽解」的對話長度變長。

　　閱讀能力測驗

　　★第一部分:「詞彙和結構」改為「詞彙」

　　★第二部分:「段落填空」(**調整選項為文意理解題**)

　　★第三部分:「閱讀理解」(**新增圖片選擇題和多文本題型**)

　　　　圖片選擇題 → **達到整合圖片和訊息的能力。**

　　　　多文本題型 → **培養整合多篇文章資訊的能力。**

　　★**總題數** 35 題 → 30 題

　　寫作能力測驗和**口說能力測驗**的題型與題數不變。

　　※詳細資訊請至全民英檢官方網站查詢。

電子朗讀音檔下載

請先輸入網址或掃描 QR code 進入「三民・東大音檔網」
https://elearning.sanmin.com.tw/Voice/

① 輸入本書書名即可找到音檔。請再依提示下載音檔。

② 也可點擊「英文」進入英文專區查找音檔後下載。

③ 若無法順利下載音檔，可至「常見問題」查看相關問題。

④ 若有音檔相關問題，請點擊「聯絡我們」，將盡快為你處理。

⑤ 更多英文新知都在臉書粉絲專頁。

Contents 目錄

TEST 9 第九回模擬試題

TEST 10 第十回模擬試題

全民英檢初級模擬試題

TEST 1

聽力測驗

第一部分　看圖辨義

第二部分　問答

第三部分　簡短對話

第四部分　短文聽解

閱讀能力測驗

第一部分　詞彙

第二部分　段落填空

第三部分　閱讀理解

寫作能力測驗

第一部分　單句寫作

第二部分　段落寫作

口說能力測驗

第一部分　複誦

第二部分　朗讀句子與短文

第三部分　回答問題

聽力測驗 ▌本測驗分四個部分，皆為單選題，共 30 題，作答時間約 20 分鐘。作答說明為中文，印在試題冊上並由音檔播出。

第一部分：看圖辨義 🔊 Track 01

共 5 題，每題請聽音檔播出題目和三個英語句子之後，選出與所看到的圖畫最相符的答案。每題只播出一遍。

A. Question 1

Answer ❶ : _____

B. Question 2

Answer ❷ : _____

C. Question 3

Gina's school Timetable

Time	Monday	Tuesday	Wednesday	Thursday	Friday
08:00-08:50	Mandarin	Science	Mandarin	Social Studies	English
09:00-09:50	Mandarin	Science	Mandarin	Social Studies	English
10:00-10:50	English	Social Studies	Math	Arts	Science
11:00-11:50	English	Social Studies	Math	Arts	Science
LUNCH TIME					
13:10-14:00	Music	PE		English	Math
14:10-15:00	Music	PE		English	Math

Answer ❸ : _____

D. Questions 4 and 5

Answer ❹ : _____   ❺ : _____

第二部分：問答 🔊 Track 02

共 10 題，每題請聽音檔播出的英語句子，再從試題冊上三個回答中，選出一個最適合的答案。每題只播出一遍。

❻ _____
A. Really? I do enjoy working in the garden.
B. Why not? It is interesting to be with kids.
C. Yes. They need to work hard.

❼ _____
A. OK. I'll speak louder.
B. Just call me when the show is over.
C. Well, I like it so much.

❽ _____
A. I used to collect it.
B. I started playing it last year.
C. No, it's easy.

❾ _____
A. No, we're going to start at four.
B. Yes, I've finished it already.
C. It's due in two weeks.

❿ _____
A. Speaking.
B. Who are you?
C. David cannot speak English.

⓫ _____
A. Really? I don't see it.
B. Just around the corner.
C. There's a bank on the fifth floor.

⓬ _____
A. That would be great.
B. OK. I'll give you the red pen.
C. Sure. Here you go.

⓭ _____
A. I think it fits alright.
B. What is it?
C. Since I was about ten.

⓮ _____
A. No, I've never been there before.
B. It's across the street.
C. That's because it serves delicious food.

⓯ _____
A. I'm going to put it up for shade.
B. I don't like to get wet.
C. That's a good idea.

第三部分：簡短對話 🔊 Track 03

共 10 題，每題請聽音檔播出一段對話和一個相關的問題後，再從試題冊
上三個選項中，選出一個最適合的答案。每段對話和問題播出一遍。

⑯ _____
  A. Her best friend.
  B. Her boyfriend.
  C. Her sister.

⑰ _____
  A. She is going to get married soon.
  B. She won a lot of money last night.
  C. She got a wonderful job yesterday.

⑱ _____
  A. Have dinner.
  B. Study.
  C. See a movie.

⑲ _____
  A. Buying something.
  B. Speaking on the phone.
  C. Studying.

⑳ _____
  A. In an airport.
  B. In a hotel.
  C. In a museum.

㉑ _____
  A. Because of her age.
  B. Because of her books.
  C. Because of her clothes.

㉒ _____
  A. She doesn't agree with the boy.
  B. She wants to hear more from the boy.
  C. She feels the same way as the boy.

㉓ _____
  A. He found her cellphone.
  B. He lost his cellphone.
  C. She called him.

㉔ _____
  A. Watched TV.
  B. Slept.
  C. Exercised.

㉕ _____
  A. He blames it on the woman.
  B. He makes an excuse.
  C. He admits his fault.

5

第四部分：短文聽解 🔊 Track 04

共 5 題，每題有三個圖片選項。請聽音檔播出的題目，並選出一個最適合的圖片。每題播出一遍。

26 _____

A.   B.   C.

27 _____

A.   B.   C.

28 _____

A.   B.   C.

29 _____

A.

B.

C.

30 _____

A.

B.

C.

閱讀能力測驗 ▎本測驗分三部分，全部都是單選題，共 30 題，作答時間 35 分鐘。

第一部分：詞彙

共 10 題，每個題目裡有一個空格。請從四個選項中選出一個最適合題意的字或詞作答。

_____ ❶ It's not your _____ for breaking the window. But be careful next time when you move something heavy.

      A. mind   B. fault   C. fun   D. reason

_____ ❷ In order to learn English well, we have to learn the _____ grammar rules.

      A. blank   B. brave   C. basic   D. bright

_____ ❸ Robert is such a selfish person that he does everything just for _____.

      A. others   B. person   C. people   D. himself

_____ ❹ I can't stand Tom anymore because he _____ to take the garbage out again.

      A. encouraged   B. decided   C. remembered   D. forgot

_____ ❺ The food I had at that fancy restaurant last night _____ so good. You should try it.

      A. handled   B. tasted   C. checked   D. prepared

_____ ❻ According to the weather forecast, we'd better _____ some water for the upcoming typhoon.

      A. light   B. save   C. fill   D. pour

_____ ❼ Justin's new album is _____ with teenagers. It is a hit this week.

      A. popular   B. bored   C. angry   D. crowded

_____ ❽ With the development of technology, it is _____ for all people to travel in outer space.

      A. comfortable   B. strange   C. possible   D. curious

_____ ❾ You never know how _____ your health is until you lose it.

      A. simple   B. ordinary   C. empty   D. important

_____ ❿ I have to study hard so as to _____ my classmates in math.

      A. catch up with   B. make friends with

      C. chat with   D. look at

第二部分：段落填空

共 8 題，包括二個段落，每個段落各含四個空格。每格均有四個選項，
請依文意選出最適合的答案。

Questions 11–14

Every morning, I enjoy riding my bicycle to school because I can see some interesting things along the road. (11) , at the bus stop, I see many students waiting for their school buses. Some students are studying, while others are chatting. Then, at the crossroads, I see a policeman waving his hands and (12) . Finally, when I ride near a park, I find people taking exercise (13) jogging or walking to keep healthy. For me, the way to school is (14) fun. That is why I like to ride to school on a bicycle.

⑪ _____
  A. In fact
  B. In other words
  C. First of all
  D. First step

⑬ _____
  A. based on
  B. such as
  C. as well as
  D. instead of

⑫ _____
  A. blowing his whistle to direct traffic
  B. driving his car to police station
  C. taking the bus to school
  D. buying a sandwich to eat

⑭ _____
  A. fill with
  B. fill of
  C. full with
  D. full of

Questions 15–18

My father works at a bank. He works five days a week, (15) Monday to Friday. He counts money and cashes checks for his (16) . He works very hard and was really busy.

However, my father does not take a rest on weekends. (17) On weekends, he cooks dinner for us. He prepares vegetable dumplings or beef noodles on Saturdays. He cooks other exotic foods on Sundays, (18) spaghetti, pizza, and steak. We all like his cooking very much and always look forward to the weekends.

⑮ _____

A. on
B. from
C. during
D. within

⑯ _____

A. patients
B. consumers
C. clients
D. companies

⑰ _____

A. He is head chef at a famous restaurant.
B. He has to do housework.
C. He goes to the bank.
D. He eats at about five o'clock.

⑱ _____

A. including
B. adding
C. having
D. borrowing

第三部分：閱讀理解

共 12 題，包括 4 個題組，每個題組含 1 至 2 篇短文，與數個相關的四選一的選擇題。請由試題冊上的選項中選出最適合的答案。

Questions 19–21

Andy's cousin, Lucy, will come to visit him. Andy plans to show her around the city. The following is "Three Days in Taipei Plan."

Friday	Saturday	Sunday
9 a.m. Morning Coffee Shop	10 a.m. Good Day Brunch	11 a.m. Maokong Gondola
3 p.m. Lungshan Temple	1 p.m. National Palace Museum	2 p.m. Taipei Zoo
7 p.m. Green Curry Noodle Hut	8 p.m. Shilin Night Market	6 p.m. 5-Star Kiln Baking Pizza

_____ **⑲** What will Lucy do on Friday afternoon?

A. Go to visit a zoo
B. Go to a museum
C. Go to visit a temple
D. Go to Shilin Night Market

_____ ⑳ When will Lucy go to visit a museum?

    A. On Friday morning

    B. On Saturday afternoon

    C. On Sunday noon

    D. On Friday night

_____ ㉑ Where will Lucy see many cute animals?

    A. Taipei Zoo

    B. Morning Coffee Shop

    C. Maokong Gondola

    D. Green Curry Noodle Hut

Questions 22–24

    In Taiwan, the seventh month of the lunar calendar is Ghost Month. People are warned of some dos and don'ts. Whether you believe them or not, you'd better follow them.

☑ **Dos**	☒ **Don'ts**
Offer food to ghosts	Get married
Burn paper money	Move into a new apartment
Say prayers for the dead	Start a new job
Release water lanterns	Travel
Offer sacrifices to ancestors	Go swimming
	Have an operation

_____ ㉒ Which of the following can be done in Ghost Month?

    A. Starting a new career

    B. Having a wedding

    C. Feeding ghosts

    D. Moving into another building

_____ ㉓ Which of the following is **NOT** a good idea during Ghost Month?

    A. Burn paper money for ghosts

    B. Visit relatives in another country

    C. Put lanterns on rivers

    D. Avoid doing surgery

_____ ㉔ What is the purpose of this article?

    A. To raise awareness about cultural taboos

    B. To warn people about the danger of releasing water lanterns

    C. To increase the importance of traditional customs

    D. To remind people of the dos and don'ts of Ghost Month

Questions 25–27

One day, a hungry dog went down the street to see if there was something to eat. Finally, he found a big bone from the **dump**. It was really something he had not had for such a long time. Then he held it between his teeth, running away quickly to enjoy the big feast.

When the dog came to a river, he saw another dog with another bone in the water. He thought if he could get the other dog's bone, then he would have two bones. What a lucky day! The other dog seemed much skinnier than him, so he might take the bone easily from the other dog. But in fact, it was simply his own reflection, yet he didn't know.

He dropped his own bone into the river when he opened his mouth, and it sank into the water. He couldn't see it anymore. At that moment, the other dog's bone was gone, too. The greedy dog suddenly realized that there was not another dog or another bone at all. He lowered his head and walked away sadly.

_____ ㉕ What does the word "**dump**" mean in the first paragraph?

A.

B.

C.

D.

㉖ Where was the bone at the end of the story?

A. Down the street   B. In the river

C. In the dog's stomach   D. Under a tree

㉗ What can we learn from the story?

A. Being greedy, you lose more.

B. Being honest, you gain less.

C. Love dogs, and dogs will love you.

D. Dogs are the best friends of human beings.

Questions 28–30

Tourists to Thailand often don't miss out the elephant show. Yet, as this business activity brings money to the country, the survival of elephants is in danger.

Since younger elephants are in favor with tourists, some people commit crimes. They catch wild baby elephants in Myanmar, keep them in small cages, and beat them cruelly to make them obey orders before selling them to Thailand. One healthy baby elephant can sell for as much as $33,000 on the black market.

Human activity has caused elephants to lose their homes and food. Besides being killed for their long teeth, they are now facing the threat of illegal wildlife trade. It's time for governments around the world to work together and stop the trade before the situation goes too far.

㉘ What is the purpose of the article?

A. To introduce the business activities in Thailand

B. To talk about the tips on keeping a baby elephant

C. To encourage people to pay a visit to Thailand

D. To ask people to save elephants

㉙ According to this article, which of the following is **NOT** a reason why elephants are hunted or killed?

A. They can perform in shows.

B. Tourists like baby elephants.

C. They damage people's houses.

D. Their long teeth can be sold.

_____ ❸⓿ According to the passage, what may tourists do to help elephants?

A. Buy more ivory products

B. Stop seeing elephant shows

C. Stop visiting Myanmar

D. Buy elephants on the black market

寫作能力測驗

第一部分：單句寫作

請將答案寫在答案欄中，如有文法、用字、拼字、標點符號、大小寫等錯誤，將予扣分。

第 1～5 題：句子改寫

請依題目之提示，將原句改寫成指定型式，並將改寫的句子**完整**地寫在答案欄中。*注意：每題均需寫出完整的句子，否則將予扣分。*

❶ Cindy went to Hong Kong yesterday.

Where _____ ?

❷ What time is it?

Tell me _____ .

❸ Dad: Did you mail the letter?

Sam: Sorry. I didn't.

Sam forgot _____ .

❹ Having a balanced diet is good for your health.

It _____ .

❺ My father punished me last night.

I was _____ .

第 6～10 題：句子合併

請依照題目指示，將兩句合併成一句，並將合併的句子**完整**地寫在答案欄中。*注意：每題均需寫出完整的句子，否則將予扣分。*

❻ Nancy is very charming.

Everyone likes Nancy.（用 so...that）

Nancy _____ .

❼ Sam is short.

Sam can play basketball well.

Although _____ .

❽ Emma complained something the other day.

We didn't hear that.

We _____.

❾ I visited Water Park.

Tanya works in Water Park.

I _____.

❿ Jimmy runs fast.

Jenny runs fast.（用 as...as）

_____.

第 11～15 題：重組

請將題目中所有提示字詞整合成一有意義的句子，並將重組的句子**完整**地寫在答案欄中。*注意：每題均需寫出完整的句子。答案中必須使用所有提示字詞，且不能隨意增減字詞及標點符號，否則不予計分。*

⓫ The groom _____.

the wedding / the bride / before / see / can't

⓬ If _____.

she can / has / for hours / a book, / read / Lucy

⓭ Angela _____.

a toy car / my birthday / gave / for / me

⓮ It's _____.

I won't / any time / something / forget / that

⓯ Cindy _____.

write / has to / her homework / for / a movie review

第二部分：段落寫作

題目：今天，Stacey 忘了帶下列圖片中的物品到學校，需要傳簡訊請媽媽送到學校給
　　　她，並與媽媽相約 12 點 10 分在校門口見。請根據提示協助 Stacey 寫一篇約
　　　50 字的簡訊給她媽媽。*注意：未依提示作答者，將予扣分。*

_____

_____

_____

_____

_____

_____

_____

_____

_____

_____

_____

口說能力測驗

🔊 Track 05

請在 15 秒內完成並唸出下列自我介紹的句子：

My seat number is （座位號碼後 5 碼）, and my test number is （考試號碼後 5 碼）.

第一部分：複誦 🔊 Track 06

共五題，經由音檔播出，每題播出兩次，兩次之間約有一至二秒的間隔。聽完兩次後，請立即複誦一次。

第二部分：朗讀句子與短文 🔊 Track 07

共有五個句子及一篇短文，請先利用一分鐘的時間閱讀句子與短文，然後在一分鐘內以正常的速度，清楚正確地朗讀一遍，閱讀時請不要發出聲音。

One:　　I don't think we've met before.

Two:　　I don't finish work until six today.

Three:　Perhaps we should try and go together.

Four:　　Do you like or hate shopping for clothes?

Five:　　As I see it, it is not polite to use bad language.

Six:　　There will be an English speech contest at Sunrise High School this Thursday. Barbara's teacher asked Barbara to enter the contest because she speaks English fluently, and her pronunciation is beautiful. Barbara is excited about it, but she's a little nervous, for she's afraid of making mistakes.

第三部分：回答問題 🔊 Track 08

共七題。經由音檔播出，每題播出兩次，兩次之間約有一至二秒的間隔。聽完兩次後，請立即回答，每題回答時間 15 秒，請在作答時間內盡量地表達。

請將下列自我介紹的句子再唸一遍：

My seat number is （座位號碼後 5 碼）, and my test number is （考試號碼後 5 碼）.

全民英檢初級模擬試題

TEST 2

聽力測驗
第一部分 看圖辨義
第二部分 問答
第三部分 簡短對話
第四部分 短文聽解

閱讀能力測驗
第一部分 詞彙
第二部分 段落填空
第三部分 閱讀理解

寫作能力測驗
第一部分 單句寫作
第二部分 段落寫作

口說能力測驗
第一部分 複誦
第二部分 朗讀句子與短文
第三部分 回答問題

聽力測驗 | 本測驗分四個部分，皆為單選題，共 30 題，作答時間約 20 分鐘。作答說明為中文，印在試題冊上並由音檔播出。

第一部分：看圖辨義 🔊 Track 09

共 5 題，每題請聽音檔播出題目和三個英語句子之後，選出與所看到的圖畫最相符的答案。每題只播出一遍。

A. Question 1

Answer ❶ : _____

B. Questions 2 and 3

Answer ❷ : _____   ❸ : _____

C. Question 4

Answer **4** : _____

D. Question 5

Answer **5** : _____

第二部分：問答 🔊 Track 10

共 10 題，每題請聽音檔播出的英語句子，再從試題冊上三個回答中，選出一個最適合的答案。每題只播出一遍。

6 _____
- A. Sure. I'll contact you by email.
- B. Yes. The one is really cool.
- C. No way. I didn't like this type of smartphone.

7 _____
- A. Say cheese!
- B. This picture is of me and my friend.
- C. That was the day we went to the zoo.

8 _____
- A. I can't tell you why he's here.
- B. Really? What level did you reach?
- C. No way. You're always the best.

9 _____
- A. Maybe I won't be there.
- B. Why don't you get up earlier?
- C. Let's get her some other things.

10 _____
- A. Why did you think of that?
- B. She is pretty good at that.
- C. I might become a teacher.

11 _____
- A. They said he is a nurse.
- B. We never talk about this.
- C. Oh, he is a decent guy.

12 _____
- A. To the countryside.
- B. With my parents.
- C. By taking the MRT.

13 _____
- A. I'll have spaghetti.
- B. That will be fine.
- C. That's no problem.

14 _____
- A. Sure. Give me your towel.
- B. Of course. What is your name?
- C. OK. Meet us here in the lobby.

15 _____
- A. Help yourself.
- B. That's my bus. Goodbye!
- C. It departs at 5:30.

第三部分：簡短對話 🔊 Track 11

共 10 題，每題請聽音檔播出一段對話和一個相關的問題後，再從試題冊上三個選項中，選出一個最適合的答案。每段對話和問題播出一遍。

⑯ _____
A. A class he took.
B. A book she has read.
C. A movie he has seen.

⑰ _____
A. A friend.
B. His girlfriend.
C. A relative.

⑱ _____
A. It is expensive.
B. The man likes its smell.
C. The woman has no list.

⑲ _____
A. To apply for a job.
B. To organize a meeting.
C. To write an essay.

⑳ _____
A. It will always look the same.
B. It will look different when it's older.
C. It will learn a lot as it grows up.

㉑ _____
A. Spring.
B. Summer.
C. Winter.

㉒ _____
A. Jenny.
B. John.
C. Mark.

㉓ _____
A. For tonight.
B. For tomorrow night.
C. For next week.

㉔ _____
A. To be nice to animals.
B. To come home earlier.
C. Not to get close to the dog.

㉕ _____
A. Sunday.
B. Monday.
C. Tuesday.

第四部分：短文聽解 🔊 Track 12

共 5 題，每題有三個圖片選項。請聽音檔播出的題目，並選出一個最適合的圖片。每題播出一遍。

26 _____

A.

B.

C.

27 _____

A.

B.

C.

28 _____

A.

B.

C.

㉙ _____

A.

B.

C.

㉚ _____

A.

B.

C.

閱讀能力測驗 ▌本測驗分三部分，全部都是單選題，共 30 題，作答時間 35 分鐘。

第一部分：詞彙

共 10 題，每個題目裡有一個空格。請從四個選項中選出一個最適合題意的字或詞作答。

_____ ❶ Students like to buy fried chicken in that store because the owner is kind and _____.

A. comfortable　　B. friendly　　　C. modern　　　D. simple

_____ ❷ Linda couldn't understand what I said, so she asked me to give her another _____.

A. business　　　B. example　　　C. knowledge　　D. menu

_____ ❸ We met Mary totally _____; we hadn't expected to meet her at all.

A. on purpose　　B. at first　　　C. with pleasure　D. by chance

_____ ❹ The Lins live in a small _____ with no dining room, so they have to have meals in the living room.

A. department　　B. town　　　　C. apartment　　D. kitchen

_____ ❺ Most of the college students have _____ English for eight or more years, haven't they?

A. arranged　　　B. learned　　　C. operated　　　D. passed

_____ ❻ There are more and more cars and motorcycles in our country, so air pollution has become a _____ problem.

A. secret　　　　B. serious　　　C. sweet　　　　D. stingy

_____ ❼ Keeping students under _____ might be a hard job for a new, young teacher.

A. control　　　　B. cover　　　　C. table　　　　D. rules

_____ ❽ We don't have enough dictionaries for each one of you, so you have to _____ them with each other.

A. follow　　　　B. prepare　　　C. share　　　　D. repeat

_____ ❾ People in cities usually go to the supermarket because it is _____ for them to buy something they need.

A. convenient　　B. excellent　　C. lucky　　　　D. ready

⑩ In my tennis class, Barbara is the only girl that _____ glasses.

    A. carries   B. wears   C. designs   D. prints

第二部分：段落填空

共 8 題，包括二個段落，每個段落各含四個空格。每格均有四個選項，請依文意選出最適合的答案。

Questions 11–14

One evening, Charlie went to the park near his house for jogging. On the way there, he found a little girl who __(11)__. "I can't find my mom!" she said. She asked Charlie __(12)__ he could help her. Charlie didn't know what to do and only said no to her __(13)__ a polite way. The little girl felt a little angry and cried out, "You __(14)__ a cold person. How can you do that to me?" Charlie turned around and ran back home quickly.

He told the whole story to his mom. "You should help her," said his mom. "I know. I was too scared at that time. Next time when I meet the little girl, I will say sorry to her," said Charlie.

⑪ _____

    A. was a police officer
    B. was happy to see him
    C. was crying for help
    D. was his good friend

⑬ _____

    A. with
    B. on
    C. by
    D. in

⑫ _____

    A. if
    B. because
    C. though
    D. until

⑭ _____

    A. are
    B. were
    C. will be
    D. would be

Questions 15–18

There's no doubt that the ten-minute breaks are the favorite time of day for students and they really make good __(15)__ of these short breaks. __(16)__, many students will rush to the playground to play sports. They play happily there. Some students will go to the school store to buy snacks because they feel __(17)__.

However, a few students choose to stay in the classroom. Some are reading novels ___(18)___ preparing for tests, while others are taking a nap to regain their energy. The ten-minute breaks are relaxing and they add color to campus life.

⑮ _____

A. money
B. progress
C. copy
D. use

⑰ _____

A. hungry
B. dirty
C. angry
D. lonely

⑯ _____

A. After the ten-minute breaks
B. Before going to school
C. On hearing the sweet ring
D. With the teacher's help

⑱ _____

A. if
B. or
C. but
D. however

第三部分：閱讀理解

共 12 題，包括 4 個題組，每個題組含 1 至 2 篇短文，與數個相關的四選一的選擇題。請由試題冊上的選項中選出最適合的答案。

Questions 19–21

CITY LIBRARY

Fun Trip	Melody
Spring is the best season to see trees and flowers. Spend a day hiking in the mountains and walking along the river to get away from your busy life.	Is music a part of your life? Read it now and enjoy different groups playing different kinds of music you've never heard before.
The Butterfly	**Tips for Cooking**
Have you ever seen any insects flying by the river? Do you know where butterflies live and what they eat? Let Judy take you into a wonderful land to visit them.	Make a fruit tart and a cup of hot black tea. Then you can have an interesting afternoon tea time with friends. Share the tips with them, you'll find more close friends around you.

_____ ⑲ Next Saturday afternoon Amy will make some cookies, and invite friends home. What is the best book for her to borrow?

A. *Fun Trip*   B. *Melody*

C. *The Butterfly*   D. *Tips for Cooking*

_____ ⑳ Lucy is going to join a rock band, so she wants to get more knowledge about pop songs. What will she need?

A. *Fun Trip*   B. *Melody*

C. *The Butterfly*   D. *Tips for Cooking*

_____ ㉑ Jimmy was asked to write a report about insects. He didn't know what to write. What do you think he might need?

A. *Fun Trip*   B. *Melody*

C. *The Butterfly*   D. *Tips for Cooking*

Questions 22–24

Have you ever thought that sunlight would pose a risk to your skin when you are enjoying it? Recent research shows that more and more people are suffering from skin cancer.

Nobody wants to get skin cancer, but for people who work outside or spend a lot of time outdoors, skin cancer is of course a risk. The good news is that it can be prevented. Wear sunscreen whenever you are outdoors in the sun, especially if you are going to the beach or working in the hot sun. Another way is to wear clothes with long sleeves, long pants, hat, and sunglasses to protect your skin from the sun. Those with light-colored skin are most in danger of having skin cancer. Follow the advice, and you will stay away from skin cancer.

_____ ㉒ What is this article mainly about?

A. How to wear sunscreen

B. Avoiding skin cancer

C. Summer fashion

D. Spending time outdoors

⑯ Which of the following is **NOT** mentioned as a way to prevent people from getting skin cancer?

A. Wear much perfume

B. Wear long pants

C. Wear sunglasses

D. Wear sunscreen

⑰ According to the article, who is in danger of getting skin cancer?

A. People who have light skins

B. People who work indoors

C. People who wear sunglasses

D. People who wear long sleeves and long pants

Questions 25–27

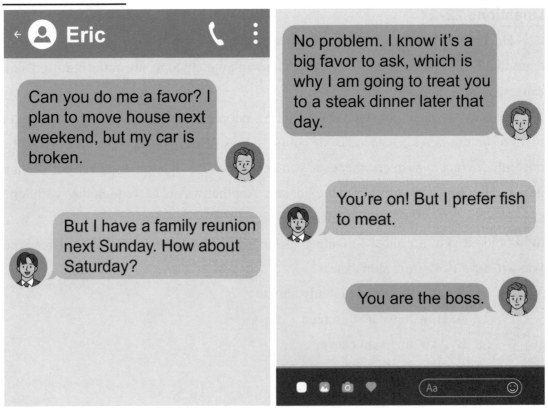

Sam will treat Eric a dinner. Below is a list of nice restaurants he found on the Internet.

Moon Café	Steak House	Mummy Hotdog	Doris Seafood
8 a.m.–12 p.m. Open every day	10 a.m.–11 p.m. 7 days a week	6 a.m.–6 p.m. Closed on Tuesdays	11 a.m.–9 p.m. Monday to Saturday

_____ ㉕ What favor does Sam ask of Eric?

    A. Helping him to repair his car

    B. Going to the family reunion with him

    C. Helping him to move house

    D. Booking a table for him

_____ ㉖ Where will they probably go to have dinner?

    A. Moon Café   B. Steak House

    C. Mummy Hotdog   D. Doris Seafood

_____ ㉗ Which of the following is true about Eric?

    A. He is available next Saturday.

    B. He will pay for their dinner.

    C. His car is under repair.

    D. He doesn't know how to drive.

Questions 28–30

Derek spent most of his free time texting people on the Internet. He liked to talk with a girl named "Sweetheart520," and she seemed to like him, too. One day, when they were talking about a newly opened amusement park, Sweetheart520 said, "Why don't we go there together? It would be fun." It gave Derek a thrill to know that he would have a chance to see her, so he answered yes quickly, and they arranged for their first meeting.

On the big day, he wore jeans and a white shirt as he promised her. He made sure everything was perfect before going out to meet her. Derek waited for her at the front gate of the amusement park. When he finally saw Sweetheart520, Derek's mind went blank. It wasn't because she was ugly or something. It was because she was his childhood friend and classmate, Meredith.

_____ 28 How did Derek often talk to Sweetheart520?

A.

B.

C.

D.

_____ 29 Why did Derek's mind go blank when he saw Sweetheart520?

A. She was as beautiful as he thought.

B. He was late for thirty minutes.

C. They had known each other since childhood.

D. The amusement park didn't open that day.

_____ 30 What is true about Meredith?

A. She went to the same school with Derek.

B. She was very ugly.

C. Someone hacked into her computer.

D. She wore jeans and a white shirt to see Derek.

寫作能力測驗 ▊

第一部分：單句寫作

請將答案寫在答案欄中，如有文法、用字、拼字、標點符號、大小寫等錯誤，將予扣分。

第 1～5 題：句子改寫

請依題目之提示，將原句改寫成指定型式，並將改寫的句子**完整**地寫在答案欄中。*注意：每題均需寫出完整的句子，否則將予扣分。*

❶ You are a very charming lady.

What _____ !

❷ Many kids are flying kites in the park.

There are _____ .

❸ I have many close friends. Lily is my close friend.

Lily is _____ .

❹ Taking care of those dogs is my duty.

It is _____ .

❺ My father plays golf twice a month.

How often _____ ?

第 6～10 題：句子合併

請依照題目指示，將兩句合併成一句，並將合併的句子**完整**地寫在答案欄中。*注意：每題均需寫出完整的句子，否則將予扣分。*

❻ Will Jimmy come on time?

I wonder that.（用 if）

I _____ .

❼ The little girl didn't know the way.

Where should the little girl go?（用 ...to + V...）

The little girl _____ .

❽ The man was killed in June.

The man's wife was pregnant in June.（用 when）

_____ .

❾ The camera is a gift from Tony.

The camera is inside the box.

_____ .

❿ My younger brother is a computer engineer. (..., a computer engineer, ...)

My younger brother works for IBM.

_____ .

第 11～15 題：重組

請將題目中所有提示字詞整合成一有意義的句子，並將重組的句子**完整**地寫在答案欄中。**注意：每題均需寫出完整的句子。答案中必須使用所有提示字詞，且不能隨意增減字詞及標點符號，否則不予計分。**

⓫ What is _____ .

to him / important / make money / the most / is

⓬ It is _____ .

big favor / of you / such a / me / to do / kind

⓭ The man _____ .

is / to walk / a rainy day / fast / in / too old

⓮ Not _____ .

did he / his visa / until / get / last Friday

⓯ I saw _____ .

the old woman / a man / her bag / of / robbing

第二部分：段落寫作

題目：F2 運動服裝店將在 11 月 11 日到 15 日舉行為期 5 天的特賣會，拍賣價格如圖示。請根據提示寫一篇約 50 字的廣告文案歡迎大家光臨。**注意：未依提示作答者，將予扣分。**

NT$250

NT$95

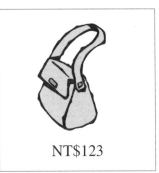
NT$123

口說能力測驗

🔊 Track 13

請在 15 秒內完成並唸出下列自我介紹的句子：

My seat number is （座位號碼後 5 碼）, and my test number is （考試號碼後 5 碼）.

第一部分：複誦 🔊 Track 14

共五題，經由音檔播出，每題播出兩次，兩次之間約有一至二秒的間隔。聽完兩次後，請立即複誦一次。

第二部分：朗讀句子與短文 🔊 Track 15

共有五個句子及一篇短文，請先利用一分鐘的時間閱讀句子與短文，然後在一分鐘內以正常的速度，清楚正確地朗讀一遍，閱讀時請不要發出聲音。

One: I'll have a cup of tea and a pack of those cookies, please.

Two: The Spanish restaurant is much nicer than the Italian one.

Three: I want a better computer than the one I have now.

Four: Do you need me to pick you up after work tonight?

Five: Let's go away for a few days next weekend.

Six: I like watching TV. Now, I'm watching a show on the ten most popular beaches in the world. The top one is bigger than the others. And there are hundreds of people on the beach. Some people are resting quietly under umbrellas. Some people are playing sand volleyball. Everybody looks very happy. How I wish I could be one of them!

第三部分：回答問題 🔊 Track 16

共七題。經由音檔播出，每題播出兩次，兩次之間約有一至二秒的間隔。聽完兩次後，請立即回答，每題回答時間 15 秒，請在作答時間內盡量地表達。

請將下列自我介紹的句子再唸一遍：

My seat number is （座位號碼後 5 碼）, and my test number is （考試號碼後 5 碼）.

全民英檢初級模擬試題
TEST 3

聽力測驗
第一部分　看圖辨義
第二部分　問答
第三部分　簡短對話
第四部分　短文聽解

閱讀能力測驗
第一部分　詞彙
第二部分　段落填空
第三部分　閱讀理解

寫作能力測驗
第一部分　單句寫作
第二部分　段落寫作

口說能力測驗
第一部分　複誦
第二部分　朗讀句子與短文
第三部分　回答問題

聽力測驗 ▌ 本測驗分四個部分,皆為單選題,共 30 題,作答時間約 20 分鐘。作答說明為中文,印在試題冊上並由音檔播出。

第一部分:看圖辨義 🔊 Track 17

共 5 題,每題請聽音檔播出題目和三個英語句子之後,選出與所看到的圖畫最相符的答案。每題只播出一遍。

A. Question 1

Answer ❶ : _____

B. Questions 2 and 3

Answer ❷ : _____   ❸ : _____

38

C. Question 4

Answer ❹ : _____

D. Question 5

Answer ❺ : _____

第二部分：問答 🔊 Track 18

共 10 題，每題請聽音檔播出的英語句子，再從試題冊上三個回答中，選出一個最適合的答案。每題只播出一遍。

❻ _____
  A. My sister bought me a pretty skirt for my birthday.
  B. Who cooks dinner for you every night?
  C. OK. By the way, can I pick the place?

❼ _____
  A. No, I often go to the movies with my friends.
  B. Yes, they are fast and convenient.
  C. Well, my favorite is ham sandwiches.

❽ _____
  A. Yes, it's lovely.
  B. Just hang them in the closet.
  C. Not at all. It's down the hall.

❾ _____
  A. About three months.
  B. Between twenty and thirty minutes.
  C. Twice a week.

❿ _____
  A. No, let's take a break!
  B. I'll just have a cup of coffee.
  C. I'm not scared.

⓫ _____
  A. I'll bring you a cup of coffee.
  B. It looks a little big on you.
  C. Sure. That's fine with me.

⓬ _____
  A. Do you have any experience?
  B. Can you help me with my résumé?
  C. About two and a half years.

⓭ _____
  A. Sure, here you are.
  B. She has been to Paris twice.
  C. I'm sorry. The book is out of stock.

⓮ _____
  A. You're welcome.
  B. How was the weather there?
  C. Didn't I tell you?

⓯ _____
  A. It could be another five minutes.
  B. Me, too. That was delicious.
  C. Smoking or non-smoking?

　　共 10 題，每題請聽音檔播出一段對話和一個相關的問題後，再從試題冊
上三個選項中，選出一個最適合的答案。每段對話和問題播出一遍。

⑯ _____
A. It's the fastest way to downtown.
B. It's really far from downtown.
C. It's faster than taking the bus.

⑰ _____
A. Two weeks.
B. Two years.
C. Two semesters.

⑱ _____
A. Basketball.
B. Volleyball.
C. Baseball.

⑲ _____
A. She got a promotion.
B. She doesn't like District 12.
C. She has to move again.

⑳ _____
A. The watch is very expensive.
B. The man bought the watch from a vendor.
C. The woman may buy a new watch from the same website.

㉑ _____
A. A place with stores.
B. A place for exercising.
C. A place to study.

㉒ _____
A. The man's.
B. The woman's.
C. The woman's sister's.

㉓ _____
A. To her office.
B. To school.
C. To the mall.

㉔ _____
A. To the bookstore.
B. To the restroom.
C. To the elevators.

㉕ _____
A. He didn't do the math homework.
B. He is good at math.
C. He has already had his breakfast.

TEST **3**

Listening

41

第四部分：短文聽解 🔊 Track 20

共 5 題，每題有三個圖片選項。請聽音檔播出的題目，並選出一個最適合的圖片。每題播出一遍。

㉖ _____

A.	B.	C.

㉗ _____

A.	B.	C.

㉘ _____

A.	B.	C.

29 _____

A.   B.   C.

30 _____

A.   B.   C.

TEST **3**

Listening

閱讀能力測驗 ▌ 本測驗分三部分，全部都是單選題，共 30 題，作答時間 35 分鐘。

第一部分：詞彙

共 10 題，每個題目裡有一個空格。請從四個選項中選出一個最適合題意的字或詞作答。

_____ ❶ My English teacher is tall and _____. She still has a good figure in her forties.

    A. handsome   B. proud   C. silent   D. slender

_____ ❷ Mom is cooking in the _____ now because my grandparents are coming for dinner.

    A. library   B. kitchen   C. museum   D. office

_____ ❸ Mary _____ to look after my pet dog while I was on vacation.

    A. invited   B. bowed   C. promised   D. examined

_____ ❹ Sophia likes reading novels and magazines very much, and she usually borrows them from the _____ near her house.

    A. bus stop   B. stationery   C. post office   D. library

_____ ❺ Christmas is coming soon. I want to buy a cellphone for my boyfriend as a _____.

    A. party   B. pleasure   C. present   D. package

_____ ❻ Mr. Wang has two daughters. _____ of them is in Taipei now. They went to Japan yesterday.

    A. One   B. Both   C. Either   D. Neither

_____ ❼ I can't tell the difference between the two watches. They are _____ in size and color.

    A. easy   B. equal   C. false   D. famous

_____ ❽ The average daily _____ last summer was 32°C, which was higher than that this year.

    A. humidity   B. temperature   C. degree   D. height

_____ ❾ The IDEAL department store is having a sale now. Let's take _____ of the sale this week and buy some clothes.

    A. advice   B. notice   C. advantage   D. amount

_____ ❿ English is a(n) _____ language. More and more people in different countries speak it.

    A. informal   B. scientific   C. beginning   D. international

第二部分：段落填空

共 8 題，包括二個段落，每個段落各含四個空格。每格均有四個選項，請依文意選出最適合的答案。

Questions 11–14

    Do you know the people in the West didn't have family names at first?　(11)　That was because more than five men　(12)　John in a small town. John didn't know　(13)　someone called him when he heard his name on the street. So he thought maybe he should give himself one more name to make sure if he was the person someone was calling. He decided to take his father's name, Jack, and put "son"　(14)　it. Then his name became John Jackson. And some people used their jobs as their family names, like Fisher, Cook and Carpenter. Some chose their favorite colors, like White and Brown. Still some got their family names from nature, like Woods and Bush. Isn't that funny?

❶❶ _____
    A. Who do you want to talk to?
    B. Why did they create their family names?
    C. How about John?
    D. What's your family name?

❶❸ _____
    A. whether
    B. why
    C. how
    D. where

❶❷ _____
    A. calling
    B. to call
    C. had called
    D. were called

❶❹ _____
    A. before
    B. over
    C. by
    D. after

Questions 15–18

   I would like to spend weekends staying home to do what I like. In the morning, I usually help my mom do some ___(15)___ , like mopping the floor, doing the laundry, and cooking breakfast for my family. ___(16)___ , I do my homework and review my lessons in my study. Later, I will listen to music and read books ___(17)___ the same time.

   In the afternoon, I will do jigsaws. ___(18)___ So, I will spend an enjoyable afternoon doing it. My family and I will watch a movie on TV or play cards together on every Saturday night. Weekends bring me much fun and I feel relaxed at home. I always look forward to the coming of every weekend.

⑮ _____
   A. housework
   B. homework
   C. schoolwork
   D. framework

⑰ _____
   A. in
   B. about
   C. on
   D. at

⑯ _____
   A. Suddenly
   B. Finally
   C. Then
   D. At first

⑱ _____
   A. It's boring to play jigsaws.
   B. I'm trying to figure out the mysterious problem.
   C. It is one of my favorite hobbies.
   D. It takes me only a few minutes.

第三部分：閱讀理解

   共 12 題，包括 4 個題組，每個題組含 1 至 2 篇短文，與數個相關的四選一的選擇題。請由試題冊上的選項中選出最適合的答案。

Questions 19–21

   In a small village, there was a quiet boy in a very poor family. His neighbors always laughed at him and called him "*fool*," but he never minded what they said. For example, when someone took out one dollar and five dollars to let the little boy decide which one he wanted, he always took one dollar, and never five dollars. One day, a kind woman thought, "Why didn't this good boy learn a lesson?" She walked up to the boy and asked him, "Why didn't you take five dollars? Don't you know it can buy more?" "Of course, I know," he said, "but they won't give me any money next time if I take five dollars. They may think I have enough money to spend. Then I'll have no more money!" Because the boy could think carefully, he finally became the ninth President of the United States, and he is William Henry Harrison.

_____ ⑲ Why didn't William take five dollars?

    A. He was afraid of his neighbors.

    B. He was far from poor.

    C. He was shy and quiet.

    D. He hoped people would give him more.

_____ ⑳ What does the word "*fool*" mean in the passage?

    A. A stupid fellow

    B. A silent boy

    C. A wise man

    D. A peace-loving person

_____ ㉑ Where was William Henry Harrison from?

    A. South Korea

    B. The United Kingdom

    C. The United States

    D. China

Questions 22–24

Sunny High School is holding a celebration for its 20th anniversary. There will be a series of activities for students and their family to attend on January 5th. Please take a look at the poster.

The ticket booth is by the right side of the gate. →→→

Tickets   NT$80 per adult   **NT$50** per student   **NT$30** per child

★ Talent show ★	★ Robot exhibition ★	★ Little photographers ★
Come to enjoy the show with us! These young students show great potential to become actors, singers, and dancers.	Come and meet the robots that play soccer! Watch them score a goal! Talk with the designer about his idea.	They see things in different angles. Vote for your favorite photographer, and the winner will receive a brand new T-6 camera.

_____ 22 If a student and his parents all want to see the talent show, how much do they have to pay in total?

A. NT$80

B. NT$130

C. NT$160

D. NT$210

_____ 23 How long does the celebration last?

A. One day

B. Twenty years

C. Two hours

D. Ninety minutes

_____ 24 According to the poster, who will play ball games?

A. Students

B. Robots

C. Photographers

D. Visitors

Questions 25–27

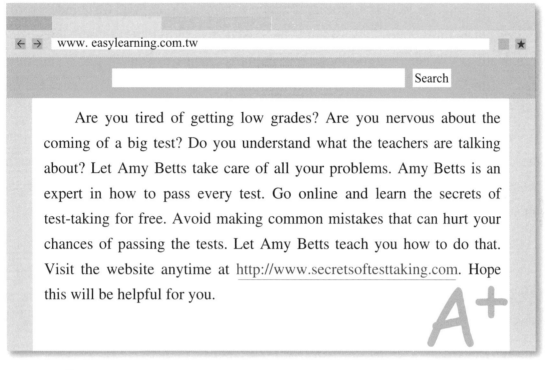

www. easylearning.com.tw

Search

Are you tired of getting low grades? Are you nervous about the coming of a big test? Do you understand what the teachers are talking about? Let Amy Betts take care of all your problems. Amy Betts is an expert in how to pass every test. Go online and learn the secrets of test-taking for free. Avoid making common mistakes that can hurt your chances of passing the tests. Let Amy Betts teach you how to do that. Visit the website anytime at http://www.secretsoftesttaking.com. Hope this will be helpful for you.

_____ ㉕ Where would you most likely read this ad?

    A. On the Internet

    B. In a library

    C. In a meeting room

    D. In a theater

_____ ㉖ When can a student get help from Amy Betts?

    A. Anytime.

    B. We don't know.

    C. When Amy has free time.

    D. After you apply for membership of the website.

_____ ㉗ How much do students have to pay for Amy's help according to the ad?

    A. It doesn't mention it

    B. As much as you like

    C. On a daily basis

    D. Without any charge

Questions 28–30

To become the leaders in the 21st century, leadership expert, Roselinde Torres, advised that three questions should be asked by individuals, companies, and organizations. "Where are you looking to the next change to your business pattern or life?" "How wide is your personal network?" "Are you brave enough to leave the old path to success and adopt new practices boldly to meet future challenges?"

In the modern world, things will be more open, digital, complicated, and international. Therefore, leaders have to come up with new ideas faster than ever in order to handle the rapid pace of change. Besides, leaders must be able to take risks. After all, they are trained to do a good job in the unknown future.

_____ ❷❽ What is this article mainly about?

        A. Useful ways to solve problems   B. Necessary leadership qualities

        C. Common interview questions   D. New challenges in the future

_____ ❷❾ According to Roselinde Torres, which of the following is a requirement of being a leader in the 21st century?

        A. Good computer skills   B. Expert knowledge

        C. A strong desire for success   D. Wide personal network

_____ ❸⓿ Where does this article most likely appear?

A.

B.

C.

D.

寫作能力測驗 ▎

第一部分：單句寫作

請將答案寫在答案欄中，如有文法、用字、拼字、標點符號、大小寫等錯誤，將予扣分。

第 1～5 題：句子改寫

請依題目之提示，將原句改寫成指定型式，並將改寫的句子**完整**地寫在答案欄中。*注意：每題均需寫出完整的句子，否則將予扣分。*

❶ The manager made me change another dish for the customer.

I was _____.

❷ The policeman said, "Do you have a driver's license?"

The policeman asked if _____.

❸ I spent one thousand dollars on the purple scarf.

It cost _____.

❹ The lazy dog is lying under the table.

Under the table _____.

❺ She seemed to have been a beauty while young.

It seemed that _____.

第 6～10 題：句子合併

請依照題目指示，將兩句合併成一句，並將合併的句子**完整**地寫在答案欄中。*注意：每題均需寫出完整的句子，否則將予扣分。*

❻ I travel around the world.

I win the lottery.

If _____.

❼ Losing weight is difficult.

Keeping fit is much more difficult.

Keeping fit _____.

❽ The boy is very smart.

The boy is very diligent.（用 ...not only...but also...）

_____.

❾ Who will be the next lucky guy?

Can you guess that?（用 Who do you guess...）

Who _____?

❿ John showed me a photo.

John took the photo at Sun Moon Lake.（用關係代名詞 that）

John _____.

第 11～15 題：重組

請將題目中所有提示字詞整合成一有意義的句子，並將重組的句子**完整**地寫在答案欄中。**注意：每題均需寫出完整的句子。答案中必須使用所有提示字詞，且不能隨意增減字詞及標點符號，否則不予計分。**

⓫ Only _____.

achieve / we / doing so / can / the goal / by

⓬ Never _____.

what / until / you can do / put off / today / tomorrow

⓭ Judy _____.

without / ahead / calling / my house / stopped by

⓮ Whether _____.

my business / is not / you / or not / help Sam

⓯ The doctor _____.

my father / should / suggested / quit smoking / that

第二部分：段落寫作

題目：昨天是聖誕節，Anna 和她的爸爸媽媽在家度過了一個美好的節日。請根據以下圖片寫一篇約 50 字的短文。**注意：未依提示作答者，將予扣分。**

_____

_____

_____

_____

_____

_____

_____

_____

_____

_____

_____

_____

口說能力測驗

🔊 Track 21

請在 15 秒內完成並唸出下列自我介紹的句子：

My seat number is （座位號碼後 5 碼）, and my test number is （考試號碼後 5 碼）.

第一部分：複誦 🔊 Track 22

共五題，經由音檔播出，每題播出兩次，兩次之間約有一至二秒的間隔。聽完兩次後，請立即複誦一次。

第二部分：朗讀句子與短文 🔊 Track 23

共有五個句子及一篇短文，請先利用一分鐘的時間閱讀句子與短文，然後在一分鐘內以正常的速度，清楚正確地朗讀一遍，閱讀時請不要發出聲音。

One: Where were you going when I saw you?

Two: You knew he had done it, didn't you?

Three: Do you want me to wash the bedroom windows?

Four: We're very close. We tell each other everything.

Five: You should have told him how you felt at that time.

Six: During the summer vacation, Tony gained 6 kilograms. He put on his jeans, but the size was too small, and he felt rather upset. Yesterday he asked his PE teacher, Ms. Baker, for help. His teacher gave him some good advice. She said, "You can lose weight by exercising. If you exercise, you sleep better. Then you'll become healthier."

第三部分：回答問題 🔊 Track 24

共七題。經由音檔播出，每題播出兩次，兩次之間約有一至二秒的間隔。聽完兩次後，請立即回答，每題回答時間 15 秒，請在作答時間內盡量地表達。

請將下列自我介紹的句子再唸一遍：

My seat number is （座位號碼後 5 碼）, and my test number is （考試號碼後 5 碼）.

全民英檢初級模擬試題
TEST 4

聽力測驗
第一部分　看圖辨義
第二部分　問答
第三部分　簡短對話
第四部分　短文聽解

閱讀能力測驗
第一部分　詞彙
第二部分　段落填空
第三部分　閱讀理解

寫作能力測驗
第一部分　單句寫作
第二部分　段落寫作

口說能力測驗
第一部分　複誦
第二部分　朗讀句子與短文
第三部分　回答問題

聽力測驗

本測驗分四個部分,皆為單選題,共 30 題,作答時間約 20 分鐘。作答說明為中文,印在試題冊上並由音檔播出。

第一部分:看圖辨義 🔊 Track 25

共 5 題,每題請聽音檔播出題目和三個英語句子之後,選出與所看到的圖畫最相符的答案。每題只播出一遍。

A. Question 1

☕ *Daisy Coffee Shop*

Drinks	Desserts
Black Tea........NT$45	Cheese Cake...NT$95
Milk Tea..........NT$60	Fruitcake.........NT$100
Black Coffee....NT$80	Cookie...........NT$25

Answer ❶ : _____

B. Question 2

Answer ❷ : _____

C. Questions 3 and 4

Answer **3** : _____ **4** : _____

D. Question 5

Answer **5** : _____

第二部分：問答 🔊 Track 26

共 10 題，每題請聽音檔播出的英語句子，再從試題冊上三個回答中，選出一個最適合的答案。每題只播出一遍。

6 _____
A. I have one question for you.
B. Thank you. I'm sure I will.
C. The room rate is one thousand per night.

7 _____
A. Delicious! I'll never forget it.
B. Why not?
C. Medium rare, please.

8 _____
A. I'll put it in my savings account.
B. I'm going to the library.
C. I can show you how to do it.

9 _____
A. Well, my company closed down.
B. I'll invite you to the party.
C. I found a new job.

10 _____
A. I suffered serious burns on my legs.
B. OK. I'll be careful.
C. You should wear more clothes.

11 _____
A. I think I can make it one more time.
B. Do they give you a better service?
C. What did the result show?

12 _____
A. I haven't seen Cindy for a long time.
B. Cindy is one of my best friends.
C. Really? I think Cindy likes Brian, too.

13 _____
A. We usually go to a nightclub.
B. They exchange presents with each other.
C. You can put up decorations.

14 _____
A. OK. I'll reserve a table.
B. Why not go to a restaurant?
C. Great! I'll call everyone.

15 _____
A. I'll have soup, please.
B. Delicious! I'll never forget it.
C. I'd like ice cream, please.

共 10 題，每題請聽音檔播出一段對話和一個相關的問題後，再從試題冊
上三個選項中，選出一個最適合的答案。每段對話和問題播出一遍。

⑯ _____

A. He became a writer.
B. He bought a book.
C. He met a special person.

⑰ _____

A. Her eyes are dark.
B. Her hair is short.
C. She is skinny.

⑱ _____

A. Some more food.
B. A flashlight.
C. Warm clothes.

⑲ _____

A. He can't read Japanese.
B. His card is not good.
C. He found the machine out of order.

⑳ _____

A. To help people without being paid.
B. To visit her sick friend.
C. To wait for her checkup results.

㉑ _____

A. It looks dangerous.
B. It looks exciting.
C. It looks old.

㉒ _____

A. His cousin.
B. His friend.
C. His classmate.

㉓ _____

A. He'll give it full consideration.
B. He'll take it for sure.
C. He doesn't think he'll take it.

㉔ _____

A. For skiing.
B. With his wife.
C. Next Friday.

㉕ _____

A. They'd like to ride on a horse.
B. They have not eaten for a while.
C. They just finished dinner.

TEST 4 Listening

第四部分：短文聽解 🔊 Track 28

共 5 題，每題有三個圖片選項。請聽音檔播出的題目，並選出一個最適合的圖片。每題播出一遍。

㉖ _____

A.

B.

C.

㉗ _____

A.

B.
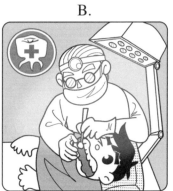

C.
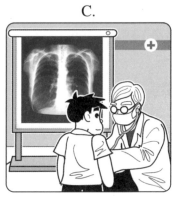

㉘ _____

A.

B.

C.

29 _____

A.

B.

C.

30 _____

A.

B.

C.

閱讀能力測驗 ▌本測驗分三部分，全部都是單選題，共 30 題，作答時間 35 分鐘。

第一部分：詞彙

共 10 題，每個題目裡有一個空格。請從四個選項中選出一個最適合題意的字或詞作答。

_____ ❶ It's _____ to wear the right clothes on the right occasion. For example, you should wear formally to the concert.

    A. polite   B. private   C. scared   D. selfish

_____ ❷ Not all of the team members agreed with your plan; _____, only a few of us wanted to support you.

    A. in fact   B. for good   C. such as   D. for example

_____ ❸ Sorry. I don't want this chicken soup because I don't eat _____.

    A. melon   B. meter   C. meat   D. metal

_____ ❹ When people have a steak, they usually use _____ and forks.

    A. chopsticks   B. spoons   C. scoops   D. knives

_____ ❺ After the fire last night, the building I worked in was _____ down.

    A. brushed   B. burnt   C. built   D. blew

_____ ❻ Tanya, I haven't been to Maokong _____. Would you like to go with me tomorrow?

    A. already   B. just   C. once   D. yet

_____ ❼ My brother always tries to scare me by telling me _____ stories.

    A. fairy   B. ghost   C. love   D. bedtime

_____ ❽ After drinking a cup of coffee, she began to tell me the plot _____.

    A. in turn   B. in detail   C. by chance   D. by mistake

_____ ❾ It _____ me three hours to fix the broken bicycle. I'm tired out now.

    A. spent   B. took   C. cost   D. paid

_____ ❿ I'm glad we have _____ views on the problem. Then we won't argue again.

    A. sincere   B. different   C. similar   D. independent

第二部分：段落填空

共 8 題，包括二個段落，每個段落各含四個空格。每格均有四個選項，請依文意選出最適合的答案。

Questions 11–14

Blackie, a much loved therapy dog, visits nursing homes every day. Once, Blackie saw an old lady ___(11)___ often looked sad and never spoke to others. It walked toward the lady and wagged its tail happily. ___(12)___ The lady patted Blackie's head and touched its back. She smiled and said, " ___(13)___ a nice dog!" All of the nurses were surprised, and some of them even cried with joy. To them, nothing is more wonderful ___(14)___ the change in the woman. It was all because Blackie helped her. As Blackie continued to visit the lady, she slowly turned into a smiling and cheerful woman.

⓫ _____
A. whom
B. whose
C. who
D. which

⓭ _____
A. How
B. What
C. So
D. It

⓬ _____
A. Then, something happened.
B. Then, bad thing happened.
C. Then, Blackie left.
D. Then, a nurse is coming.

⓮ _____
A. for
B. as
C. but
D. than

Questions 15–18

Over the past few years, global warming has become more and more serious. What can we do to help our planet? The first step we can ___(15)___ is to grow as many trees as possible. That is because trees can help reduce global warming. ___(16)___ useful step is to take public transportation such as trains, buses, and MRT more often. ___(17)___ we can cut the greenhouse gas emissions. The third one is that we can take the stairs instead of the elevators, which ___(18)___ . As long as we work together, I deeply believe that the problem of global warming may be solved someday.

⑮ _____
- A. learn
- B. do
- C. take
- D. go

⑯ _____
- A. Another
- B. Other
- C. Some
- D. Any

⑰ _____
- A. Likewise
- B. Thus
- C. However
- D. Rarely

⑱ _____
- A. helps us grow trees
- B. spends a lot of money
- C. is the root cause of global warming
- D. helps us save energy and keeps us healthy

第三部分：閱讀理解

共 12 題，包括 4 個題組，每個題組含 1 至 2 篇短文，與數個相關的四選一的選擇題。請由試題冊上的選項中選出最適合的答案。

Questions 19–21

10/23 ☼

Next Saturday is Halloween. I am really looking forward to it. My best friend, John, told me that he would dress up as a vampire. And I would like to dress up as a witch. So John and I met at Alex's Halloween Joke Store this morning. Because I've already had a witch's hat and some candy fingers, I only bought a jumping spider. And John bought a set of vampire teeth and a pair of fake bats. Thanks to John's VIP card, we got a twenty percent discount on all of the goods.

_____ ❶❾ What day did Peggy and John go to Alex's Halloween Joke Store?

    A. Thursday

    B. Friday

    C. Saturday

    D. Sunday

_____ ❷⓪ What is **NOT** included in Peggy's witch costume?

    A. A fake bat

    B. Some candy fingers

    C. A jumping spider

    D. A witch's hat

_____ ㉑ How much did John spend on his costume at Alex's Halloween Joke Store?

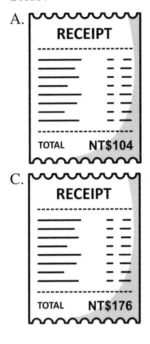

A.

RECEIPT

TOTAL   NT$104

B.

RECEIPT

TOTAL   NT$130

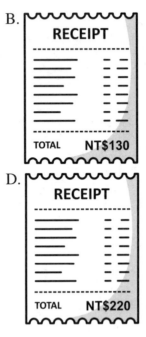

C.

RECEIPT

TOTAL   NT$176

D.

RECEIPT

TOTAL   NT$220

Questions 22–24

When walking your dog in public places, please be sure to pick up after your dog when it does its "business." We have received complaints from residents of this community about the sight and smell of waste left on the streets and sidewalks. It's as easy as bringing a plastic bag with you. Use the plastic bag to clean up any waste your dog has left behind. It's an easy, no-mess solution that everyone can do. From now on, pet owners will be fined up to NT$5,000 by the community committee if they don't clean up after their pets.

The last but not the least, due to water shortages, the swimming pool is closed until further notice.

_____ ㉒ What is this notice mainly about?

    A. Don't walk your dog in public places.

    B. Pick up after your pet.

    C. Dog owners need to buy plastic bags.

    D. Swimming in the swimming pool will be fined for NT$5,000.

_____ ㉓ What will happen if dog owners don't clean up after their dogs?

    A. They will receive complaints.

    B. They will have to clean up the mess.

    C. They will get bitten.

    D. They will be fined.

_____ ㉔ Who is most likely to post this notice?

    A. The police

    B. The pet owners

    C. The community committee

    D. The dog trainers

Questions 25–27

It is believed that a good start is halfway to success. The twenties are often regarded as the most precious stage of one's life. These young adults will have several important decisions to make, such as whether to continue higher study or to start one's career. Here are some tips which may benefit them in the near future.

As they start to figure out what the real world is like beyond the walls of school, they may ask themselves questions like, "What can interest me the most?" or "What are my strong and weak points?" To choose the right path of success, these young adults have to keep asking questions and learning from their mistakes. In addition, young adults are also advised to take trips to experience different cultures.

_____ ㉕ How does the author begin this article?

    A. By offering advice

    B. By giving an old saying

    C. By comparing people's opinions

    D. By asking several questions

_____ ❷❻ According to this article, what may trouble young adults?

    A. Whether they should have higher education

    B. Whom they should go out on a date with

    C. Which school activity they should take part in

    D. Whether they should find a part-time job

_____ ❷❼ According to this article, which of the following is **NOT** a way to help young adults choose the right path of success?

    A. Learning from their mistakes

    B. Traveling to experience different cultures

    C. Finding out their interests

    D. Asking their parents for advice

Questions 28–30

Home > Life > Food

Fruits and Vegetables: Prevent Disease?

By Pam Brown

    Fruits and vegetables are good for your body. That's why everyone says "Eat more fruits and vegetables." They make your body healthy. Your body gets vitamins from them as well. They can also prevent diseases. Here are some examples:

- Apples: The red, green or yellow fruit can help you in many ways. Apples have plenty of vitamin C in them. As a saying goes, "An apple a day keeps the doctor away." So just eat an apple a day.
- Broccoli: Eat more dark green broccoli. Eating it can prevent heart disease and cancer.
- Carrots: Carrots offer much vitamin A, B, and C. They contain more vitamin A than other vegetables.
- Spinach: Eating spinach can keep your hair and skin healthy. The vitamin K in spinach also keeps your bones healthy.

1 | 2   **NEXT PAGE >>**

More articles in Food >>

28 What is this online article mainly about?

    A. Lack of vitamins may make you sick.

    B. Fruits and vegetables are good for your body.

    C. Eating more apples makes you pretty.

    D. We should listen to what the doctor says.

29 What can dark green vegetables do to help?

    A. Provide vitamin K

    B. Keep you fit

    C. Prevent heart disease

    D. Lose weight

30 Which of the following statements is **NOT** true?

    A. Carrots provide more vitamin A than other vegetables.

    B. Apples contain a high amount of vitamin C.

    C. Spinach is good for hair, skins and bones.

    D. Broccoli is dark green and can protect your eyes.

寫作能力測驗

第一部分：單句寫作

請將答案寫在答案欄中，如有文法、用字、拼字、標點符號、大小寫等錯誤，將予扣分。

第 1～5 題：句子改寫

請依題目之提示，將原句改寫成指定型式，並將改寫的句子**完整**地寫在答案欄中。**注意：每題均需寫出完整的句子，否則將予扣分。**

❶ My mother spent one hour cleaning the kitchen.

It _____ .

❷ A good student seldom skips classes.

Seldom _____ .

❸ Cindy fell off her bike in the park.

It was in the park _____ .

❹ Let's go downstairs and watch TV!

What about _____ ?

❺ Before going to bed, brush your teeth.

After _____ .

第 6～10 題：句子合併

請依照題目指示，將兩句合併成一句，並將合併的句子**完整**地寫在答案欄中。**注意：每題均需寫出完整的句子，否則將予扣分。**

❻ I eat something before going to sleep.

I have gotten used to it.（用 get used to）

_____ .

❼ David was late for school.

David didn't catch the school bus.（用 because）

_____ .

❽ The girl moved to Paris in 2014.

The girl still lives in Paris now.（用 since）

_____ .

❾ Simon is Lucy's student.

Lucy has many students.

Simon _____.

❿ Tina didn't steal the money.

Tina insisted that.

Tina insisted _____.

第 11～15 題：重組

　　請將題目中所有提示字詞整合成一有意義的句子，並將重組的句子**完整**地寫在答案欄中。*注意：每題均需寫出完整的句子。答案中必須使用所有提示字詞，且不能隨意增減字詞及標點符號，否則不予計分。*

⓫ I _____.

on weekends / to do / homework/ a lot of / have

⓬ Jenny _____.

her son / standing up / was / to see / surprised

⓭ We'd _____.

not tell / immediately / the truth / them / better

⓮ The woman _____.

preparing dinner / in the kitchen / was / busy

⓯ Don't _____.

for you / can do / others/ ask / what

第二部分：段落寫作

題目：暑假你要去加拿大渡假。請根據以下圖片寫一篇約 50 字的旅行計劃。 *注意：*
   未依提示作答者，將予扣分。

口說能力測驗

🔊 Track 29

請在 15 秒內完成並唸出下列自我介紹的句子：

My seat number is （座位號碼後 5 碼）, and my test number is （考試號碼後 5 碼）.

第一部分：複誦 🔊 Track 30

共五題，經由音檔播出，每題播出兩次，兩次之間約有一至二秒的間隔。聽完兩次後，請立即複誦一次。

第二部分：朗讀句子與短文 🔊 Track 31

共有五個句子及一篇短文，請先利用一分鐘的時間閱讀句子與短文，然後在一分鐘內以正常的速度，清楚正確地朗讀一遍，閱讀時請不要發出聲音。

One: Would you mind having the chicken instead?

Two: I'd like to work in the media because the job must be exciting.

Three: It really bothers me when people smoke in restaurants.

Four: Honestly, I would if I could, but I can't.

Five: I'd rather use a knife and fork than chopsticks.

Six: Every day we take important resources from the earth, such as wood, water, and oil. At the same time, we do harm to it as well. Our factories, vehicles, and garbage are polluting the air, water, and land. If we don't take measures and do something, soon there will be no trees, no clean water, and no food. How terrible!

第三部分：回答問題 🔊 Track 32

共七題。經由音檔播出，每題播出兩次，兩次之間約有一至二秒的間隔。聽完兩次後，請立即回答，每題回答時間 15 秒，請在作答時間內盡量地表達。

請將下列自我介紹的句子再唸一遍：

My seat number is （座位號碼後 5 碼）, and my test number is （考試號碼後 5 碼）.

全民英檢初級模擬試題
TEST 5

聽力測驗
第一部分 看圖辨義
第二部分 問答
第三部分 簡短對話
第四部分 短文聽解

閱讀能力測驗
第一部分 詞彙
第二部分 段落填空
第三部分 閱讀理解

寫作能力測驗
第一部分 單句寫作
第二部分 段落寫作

口說能力測驗
第一部分 複誦
第二部分 朗讀句子與短文
第三部分 回答問題

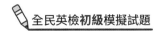

聽力測驗 ▌ 本測驗分四個部分,皆為單選題,共 30 題,作答時間約 20 分鐘。作答說明為中文,印在試題冊上並由音檔播出。

第一部分:看圖辨義 🔊 Track 33

共 5 題,每題請聽音檔播出題目和三個英語句子之後,選出與所看到的圖畫最相符的答案。每題只播出一遍。

A. Question 1

Jane Smith		
	EDUCATION	San Min University Dept. of Marketing
	SKILLS	social media marketing, creativity
	LANGUAGES	English, Japanese, Spanish
CONTACT ✉ janesmith@smail.com ☎ 0912-345-xxx	HOBBIES	reading, swimming, cycling

Answer ❶ : _____

B. Question 2

Answer ❷ : _____

C. Questions 3 and 4

Answer ❸ : _____   ❹ : _____

D. Question 5

Answer ❺ : _____

第二部分：問答 🔊 Track 34

共 10 題，每題請聽音檔播出的英語句子，再從試題冊上三個回答中，選出一個最適合的答案。每題只播出一遍。

6 _____
A. So do I.
B. Neither do I.
C. Nor can I.

7 _____
A. I don't like her either.
B. Will you go shopping with Judy this weekend?
C. No wonder no one knows her well.

8 _____
A. You need to go to see a doctor.
B. I'll stay in the hospital for a while.
C. Your dad is a really nice doctor.

9 _____
A. Well, he is a famous baseball player.
B. Oh, yes. Do you like basketball, too?
C. No, he didn't. That's interesting!

10 _____
A. I'm starting a new job on Monday.
B. I'm sorry to hear that.
C. Good luck!

11 _____
A. A few, please.
B. None, thanks.
C. Fish, please.

12 _____
A. I know. I feel so good now.
B. Yes. I enjoy doing yoga.
C. Oh, stop making fun of me.

13 _____
A. Oh, great. I had a lot of fun there.
B. No, it's bigger than Taiwan.
C. That's right. I went to some of the best beaches.

14 _____
A. Tina's is much brighter.
B. My room is darker than yours.
C. I think Eric's room is the largest.

15 _____
A. No, I don't think so.
B. She sings well, but she has a bad cold.
C. My name is Jenny Cook.

共 10 題，每題請聽音檔播出一段對話和一個相關的問題後，再從試題冊上三個選項中，選出一個最適合的答案。每段對話和問題播出一遍。

⑯ _____
A. Checking in.
B. Checking out.
C. Reserving a room.

⑰ _____
A. Because the woman phones the restaurant in advance.
B. Because the man knows the manager of the restaurant.
C. Because the restaurant won't cancel people's reservation easily.

⑱ _____
A. He didn't like Lucy.
B. He forgot to call Lucy.
C. He didn't know the woman was Lucy at first.

⑲ _____
A. Two o'clock in the afternoon.
B. Seven o'clock at night.
C. Seven o'clock in the morning.

⑳ _____
A. Her new apartment.
B. His new house.
C. Their new office.

㉑ _____
A. She asks the man to run with her.
B. She's sure the man can make it.
C. She doesn't worry about the man.

㉒ _____
A. To have a checkup.
B. To work for Dr. Lin.
C. To ask her questions.

㉓ _____
A. She needs to pick up Ted.
B. Ted is in danger.
C. She is scared of Ted.

㉔ _____
A. Continue reading.
B. Go to the theater.
C. Talk to the man.

㉕ _____
A. Play basketball.
B. Play video games.
C. Go to a baseball game.

TEST 5

Listening

第四部分：短文聽解 🔊 Track 36

共 5 題，每題有三個圖片選項。請聽音檔播出的題目，並選出一個最適合的圖片。每題播出一遍。

㉖ _____

A.
B.
C.

㉗ _____

A.
B.
C.

㉘ _____

A.
B.
C.

㉙ _____

A.

B.

C.

㉚ _____

A.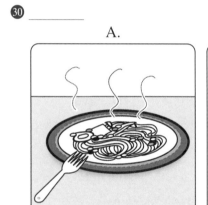

B.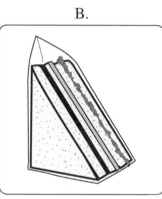

C.

閱讀能力測驗 ┃ 本測驗分三部分,全部都是單選題,共 30 題,作答時間 35 分鐘。

第一部分:詞彙

共 10 題,每個題目裡有一個空格。請從四個選項中選出一個最適合題意的字或詞作答。

_____ ❶ As the department store is having a big sale, we can buy what we need at _____ prices.

A. higher　　　　B. less　　　　C. fewer　　　　D. lower

_____ ❷ John is not good at sports. It is always a big _____ for him to play basketball, baseball, or volleyball.

A. difference　　B. headache　　C. confusion　　D. lesson

_____ ❸ My father always drives to work, but _____ he takes a bus.

A. usually　　　B. seldom　　　C. sometimes　　D. never

_____ ❹ Maybe we have the last _____ to escape from here. Why don't we try it?

A. example　　　B. chance　　　C. experience　　D. habit

_____ ❺ Would you please _____ the radio? The baby is sleeping.

A. turn over　　B. turn in　　　C. turn down　　D. turn up

_____ ❻ Don't you remember your father's birthday is _____ October 21st?

A. at　　　　　B. in　　　　　C. of　　　　　D. on

_____ ❼ Lisa is _____ of darkness, so she never stays at home alone.

A. afraid　　　B. proud　　　C. mad　　　　D. kind

_____ ❽ Double Tenth Day is our national _____. We have no school that day.

A. hero　　　　B. history　　　C. tradition　　D. holiday

_____ ❾ Andrew likes music very much. He often plays the _____ after he finishes doing his homework.

A. basketball　　　　　　　　　B. computer game

C. violin　　　　　　　　　　　D. cat

_____ ❿ It will be interesting to see how Dave is going to _____ his new boss.

A. get back to　　B. get around to　　C. get along with　　D. get away with

82

第二部分：段落填空

共8題，包括二個段落，每個段落各含四個空格。每格均有四個選項，請依文意選出最適合的答案。

Questions 11–14

Everyone knows that motorcycles are very convenient. However, people usually   (11)   ignore the fact that it can be dangerous, too.   (12)   On a rainy day, a terrible traffic accident happened to Jean. She   (13)   by a truck while riding her motorcycle to go to work in a hurry. Unfortunately, her legs were so seriously injured that the doctor had to cut them off. To her sorrow, she had to be in a wheelchair for   (14)   her life. The accident has totally changed her life. She can't walk, run, and dance again. Let that be a lesson to all of us. We should remember that safety always comes first and never hurry on a motorcycle.

⑪ _____
- A. tend to
- B. decide to
- C. hope to
- D. agree to

⑫ _____
- A. Take Jean for example.
- B. Take it or leave it.
- C. It's convenient for Jean to ride a motorcycle.
- D. It will be safe to ride a motorcycle.

⑬ _____
- A. hit
- B. hitting
- C. was hit
- D. has been hit

⑭ _____
- A. the end of
- B. the rest of
- C. the last of
- D. the real of

Questions 15–18

Last weekend, my class went to Happy Zoo by bus. It was about ten o'clock when we arrived. We went to the children's section first   (15)   some of my classmates wanted to interact with the elephants. I was more interested   (16)   petting the sheeps, though.   (17) , we went to see the little sharks. While we were there, it was   (18)   time. We watched the sharks eating fish out of the trainer's hands. The sharks swam here and there and played with each other. It was an unforgettable experience for all of us.

⑮ _____

A. when
B. until
C. because
D. then

⑯ _____

A. at
B. in
C. with
D. of

⑰ _____

A. After we visited the children's
   section
B. Last but not least
C. Before we went to see the elephant
D. While we swam in the pool

⑱ _____

A. sleeping
B. playing
C. showing
D. feeding

第三部分：閱讀理解

共 12 題，包括 4 個題組，每個題組含 1 至 2 篇短文，與數個相關的四選一的選擇題。請由試題冊上的選項中選出最適合的答案。

Questions 19–21

✉   ─ ⌐⌐ ✕

To: Mom <janesmith@gmail.com>

Subject: Arrived in New York City safely

Dear Mom,

I arrived safely in New York City yesterday. Uncle Ben picked me up at the airport. When we got in the car, it was freezing cold outside. It never gets that cold in Taipei. I was glad you made me bring the coat, a pair of gloves, and the woolen scarf.

When I woke up in the morning, there was snow outside the window. It was beautiful and peaceful. In the afternoon, I went sledding with cousin David and cousin Alice, and we had a snowball fight. It was so much fun! Even though I wore my heavy fur gloves, my hands were still frozen. What's more, I am going to a Christmas party with Alice tomorrow night and I really can't wait!

Please don't worry about me. Everything is great. I think this is going to be the best vacation I have ever had.

Love,
Lisa

⑲ According to the email, what season was it in New York City?

A. Spring

B. Summer

C. Fall

D. Winter

⑳ What did it look like outside when Lisa woke up in the morning?

A. It was dirty.

B. It was warm.

C. It was thriving.

D. It was white.

㉑ Which of the following statements is true?

A. Lisa goes to New York City with her friends.

B. Taipei is as cold as New York City.

C. Alice goes to the Christmas party alone.

D. David is a close relative of Lisa.

Questions 22–24

Mattie Stepanek died on June 22, 2004. He was thirteen years old. Mattie had muscular dystrophy. Because two of his brothers and one sister died from the same illness, Mattie knew a lot about sadness and death. However, his books are full of love and beauty. Flowers, trees, and stars are more alive in his poetry. People can even smell rainbows and taste the sky in his books. Although Mattie was a little boy, he said that fighting is wrong and the most important things in life are friendship and happiness.

Mattie's books are a reminder that life is precious and we should enjoy it no matter we are young, old, sick or healthy. We should all remember that Mattie is not only a writer but also a fighter.

㉒ What did Mattie know about?

A. Madness and being deaf

B. Sadness and death

C. Being healthy

D. Being gifted

㉓ What do we know about Mattie?

A. He believed that war was right.

B. He suffered from depression.

C. He was a little poet.

D. He was thirty years old when he died.

㉔ How many people in Mattie's family have died from muscular dystrophy?

A. Two brothers and one sister

B. Two sisters and one brother

C. Three sisters and two brothers

D. Three brothers and two sisters

Questions 25–27

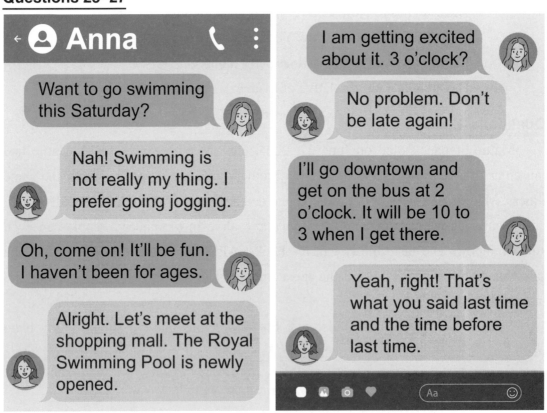

Anna

Want to go swimming this Saturday?

Nah! Swimming is not really my thing. I prefer going jogging.

Oh, come on! It'll be fun. I haven't been for ages.

Alright. Let's meet at the shopping mall. The Royal Swimming Pool is newly opened.

I am getting excited about it. 3 o'clock?

No problem. Don't be late again!

I'll go downtown and get on the bus at 2 o'clock. It will be 10 to 3 when I get there.

Yeah, right! That's what you said last time and the time before last time.

Aa

Helen is going to hang out with Anna this Saturday. Below is the information about downtown buses she found on the Internet.

Bus Services from Downtown

From Downtown to	Distance	Journey Time	Bus Fare
South Station	6 km	20 mins	NT$15
Long Beach	10 km	50 mins	NT$30
Sixth Avenue	20 km	70 mins	NT$45

_____ ㉕ What will Helen and Anna do this Saturday?

A.

B.

C.

D.

_____ ㉖ Where is the shopping mall probably located in?

A. Long Beach

B. South Station

C. Sixth Avenue

D. Downtown

_____ ㉗ What do we know about Helen?

A. She goes swimming every week.

B. She is often late for meetings.

C. She lives near the Royal Swimming Pool.

D. She likes to go jogging.

Questions 28–30

Memory problems can result from bad habits, and many people believe that developing good habits is the key to a better memory. There are many tips for improving one's memory. For example, it is important to set realistic goals and focus on the areas that need the most work. Another way to keep one's memory sharp is to stay mentally active by exercising the mind with mental challenges.

Reading more is an excellent way to exercise the brain, and it also helps to improve one's vocabulary, which is an effective way to improve memory. Finally, sharing knowledge with others is perhaps the best way to remember things because it requires a person to review what he knows and express it to others. All of these tips are useful in creating good mental habits, but everyone must find their own unique combination for success.

_____ ㉘ According to the article, what causes memory loss?

      A. Reading

      B. Bad habit

      C. Exercise

      D. Mental challenge

_____ ㉙ Which of the following tips for improving memory is **NOT** mentioned in the passage?

      A. Creating new words

      B. Doing mental challenges to exercise the mind

      C. Sharing knowledge with other people

      D. Reading many books

_____ ㉚ What can people learn from this article?

      A. What is the best method for reading

      B. How memory is being used

      C. How to improve reading skills

      D. How to enhance memory

寫作能力測驗 ▌

第一部分：單句寫作

請將答案寫在答案欄中，如有文法、用字、拼字、標點符號、大小寫等錯誤，將予扣分。

第 1～5 題：句子改寫

請依題目之提示，將原句改寫成指定型式，並將改寫的句子**完整**地寫在答案欄中。**注意：*每題均需寫出完整的句子，否則將予扣分。***

❶ A man is standing in front of the bus.

In front of _____.

❷ When will Tom leave?

I have no idea _____.

❸ To get good grades is not easy.

It _____.

❹ I met Maggie on the plane yesterday.

Where _____?

❺ Mom made me wipe the table after dinner.

I _____.

第 6～10 題：句子合併

請依照題目指示，將兩句合併成一句，並將合併的句子**完整**地寫在答案欄中。**注意：*每題均需寫出完整的句子，否則將予扣分。***

❻ The man is poor.

The man is happy. (Although...)

_____.

❼ Chris enjoys something.

Chris jumps up and down on the sofa.

_____.

❽ Harry bought flowers.

The flowers are for Teresa.

_____.

❾ Jimmy is 180 centimeters tall.

Kevin is 180 centimeters, too. (as...as...)

_____.

❿ You are right.

I'm right, too. (and so...)

_____.

第 11～15 題：重組

請將題目中所有提示字詞整合成一有意義的句子，並將重組的句子**完整**地寫在答案欄中。*注意：每題均需寫出完整的句子。答案中必須使用所有提示字詞，且不能隨意增減字詞及標點符號，否則不予計分。*

⓫ Could _____?

please / do me / now / you / a favor

⓬ My _____.

the river / sister / swim / across / is able to

⓭ Billy _____.

on foot / school / usually / goes to

⓮ How _____?

to / last trip / was / your / Disneyland

⓯ Dad _____.

up / me / this afternoon / at five o'clock / will pick

題目：請根據以下圖片寫一篇約 50 字關於草莓牛奶的製作過程。 *注意：未依提示作答者，將予扣分。*

_____

_____

_____

_____

_____

_____

_____

_____

_____

_____

_____

_____

_____

_____

_____

TEST 5 Writing

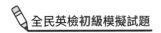
口說能力測驗

🔊 Track 37

請在 15 秒內完成並唸出下列自我介紹的句子：

My seat number is （座位號碼後 5 碼）, and my test number is （考試號碼後 5 碼）.

第一部分：複誦 🔊 Track 38

共五題，經由音檔播出，每題播出兩次，兩次之間約有一至二秒的間隔。聽完兩次後，請立即複誦一次。

第二部分：朗讀句子與短文 🔊 Track 39

共有五個句子及一篇短文，請先利用一分鐘的時間閱讀句子與短文，然後在一分鐘內以正常的速度，清楚正確地朗讀一遍，閱讀時請不要發出聲音。

One: You've given up smoking, haven't you?

Two: I thought it was the best movie I've ever seen.

Three: I wish I'd majored in a different subject.

Four: Oh no! We should have been there half an hour ago!

Five: You have to take the dog for a walk every day.

Six: Mother's Day is on the second Sunday in May. On this day, people try to do something special to show their love for their mothers. Some children give cards or gifts to their mothers. They may also take Mom out to her favorite restaurants for dinner. It's a happy day for mothers, but don't forget to say, "Mom, I love you!"

第三部分：回答問題 🔊 Track 40

共七題。經由音檔播出，每題播出兩次，兩次之間約有一至二秒的間隔。聽完兩次後，請立即回答，每題回答時間 15 秒，請在作答時間內盡量地表達。

請將下列自我介紹的句子再唸一遍：

My seat number is （座位號碼後 5 碼）, and my test number is （考試號碼後 5 碼）.

全民英檢初級模擬試題
TEST 6

聽力測驗
第一部分　看圖辨義
第二部分　問答
第三部分　簡短對話
第四部分　短文聽解

閱讀能力測驗
第一部分　詞彙
第二部分　段落填空
第三部分　閱讀理解

寫作能力測驗
第一部分　單句寫作
第二部分　段落寫作

口說能力測驗
第一部分　複誦
第二部分　朗讀句子與短文
第三部分　回答問題

聽力測驗 ▍本測驗分四個部分，皆為單選題，共 30 題，作答時間約 20 分鐘。作答說明為中文，印在試題冊上並由音檔播出。

第一部分：看圖辨義 🔊 Track 41

共 5 題，每題請聽音檔播出題目和三個英語句子之後，選出與所看到的圖畫最相符的答案。每題只播出一遍。

A. Questions 1 and 2

Answer ❶ : _____ ❷ : _____

B. Question 3

EAST TO
New York City
LEFT 1/2 MILE

Answer ❸ : _____

C. Question 4

Answer **4** : _____

D. Question 5

Answer **5** : _____

第二部分：問答 🔊 Track 42

共 10 題，每題請聽音檔播出的英語句子，再從試題冊上三個回答中，選出一個最適合的答案。每題只播出一遍。

⑥ _____
A. I'll have some ice cream.
B. They're too short.
C. That was exciting.

⑦ _____
A. It matters a lot to me.
B. I had a fight with my brother.
C. What's up?

⑧ _____
A. You should go on a diet.
B. How about trying to eat more?
C. I think you're a good writer.

⑨ _____
A. It's too small, right?
B. I know. It looks great on me.
C. Yes, I should get a few in this size.

⑩ _____
A. I went to get a visa for my trip.
B. Of course. You're leaving tomorrow.
C. Yes, I'll book a ticket first.

⑪ _____
A. Yes, I have been to Disneyland.
B. No, I haven't. But my cousin has.
C. Yes, she's always traveling.

⑫ _____
A. I'll try that now. Thanks.
B. My printer doesn't work.
C. Sure. What's the problem?

⑬ _____
A. Anne is in Japan now.
B. I've never been there before.
C. That sounds great. How about going to Kenting?

⑭ _____
A. That is the reason I like it.
B. I think it will help me find a job.
C. I prefer the yellow one.

⑮ _____
A. Neither can I.
B. Does she? I hate it!
C. So do I.

第三部分：簡短對話 🔊 Track 43

共 10 題，每題請聽音檔播出一段對話和一個相關的問題後，再從試題冊上三個選項中，選出一個最適合的答案。每段對話和問題播出一遍。

⑯ _____
A. Very soon.
B. At four.
C. In an hour.

⑰ _____
A. He was stuck in heavy traffic.
B. His car was broken.
C. He was watching a baseball game.

⑱ _____
A. The teacher was strict.
B. It was easy to complete the assignment.
C. There was too much homework.

⑲ _____
A. It is boring.
B. It is not an outdoor activity.
C. It is too hard.

⑳ _____
A. A friend of the man's mother.
B. The male speaker's dog.
C. The woman's dog.

㉑ _____
A. A raincoat.
B. A hat.
C. A bicycle.

㉒ _____
A. The woman will call her manager.
B. The man will walk out of the store.
C. The woman will buy this coat.

㉓ _____
A. It is too large.
B. It is too tight.
C. It is too expensive.

㉔ _____
A. In a restaurant.
B. In a garage.
C. At the mall.

㉕ _____
A. Spring.
B. Summer.
C. Fall.

第四部分：短文聽解 🔊 Track 44

共 5 題，每題有三個圖片選項。請聽音檔播出的題目，並選出一個最適合的圖片。每題播出一遍。

26 _____

A.

B.

C.

27 _____

A.

B.

C.

28 _____

A.

B.

C.

㉙ _____

A.

B.

C.

㉚ _____

A.

B.

C.

閱讀能力測驗

本測驗分三部分，全部都是單選題，共 30 題，作答時間 35 分鐘。

第一部分：詞彙

共 10 題，每個題目裡有一個空格。請從四個選項中選出一個最適合題意的字或詞作答。

_____ ❶ My brother is a baseball fan, so I bought him a baseball _____ as his 10th birthday present.

    A. glass   B. glove   C. goat   D. grass

_____ ❷ Autumn is the best _____ in a year. It won't be too cold or too hot.

    A. season   B. sentence   C. month   D. weather

_____ ❸ I hope that you have learned a _____ from this experience.

    A. lesson   B. score   C. tip   D. recipe

_____ ❹ A common language is a _____ between different cultures. So learning languages is very important.

    A. umbrella   B. island   C. bridge   D. bottom

_____ ❺ Things made by machine are usually much cheaper than _____ made by hand.

    A. it   B. this   C. ones   D. those

_____ ❻ Jessica made a chocolate cake in the _____ of a heart for her boyfriend.

    A. spirit   B. shape   C. middle   D. limit

_____ ❼ May and I have the same interest and _____. We both like dancing.

    A. direction   B. fortune   C. level   D. hobby

_____ ❽ Don't worry. I'll _____ Ken from school. We'll be home around seven.

    A. give up   B. make up   C. look up   D. pick up

_____ ❾ Tony seldom _____ his homework on time, does he?

    A. hands in   B. holds up   C. puts away   D. reads over

_____ ❿ Not until we lose our friends do we know the value of _____.

    A. leadership   B. friendship   C. shoulder   D. stranger

第二部分：段落填空

共 8 題，包括二個段落，每個段落各含四個空格。每格均有四個選項，
請依文意選出最適合的答案。

Questions 11–14

In Western countries, people usually shake hands when meeting ___(11)___ the first time. This practice is common for both men and women. A handshake should be neither too hard ___(12)___ too soft, and the right hand—never the left hand—is always used.

Close friends or family members will often ___(13)___ when meeting and saying goodbye. In many European countries, kissing each other lightly on both cheeks ___(14)___ common. In native English-speaking countries, however, this is not common practice.

⑪ _____
    A. for
    B. at
    C. in
    D. with

⑫ _____
    A. and
    B. or
    C. but
    D. nor

⑬ _____
    A. shake people's hand
    B. bow our heads in prayer
    C. hug and kiss each other
    D. give each other a wave

⑭ _____
    A. are
    B. is
    C. does
    D. did

Questions 15–18

Nowadays we tend to get tired from heavy workload. So, it is important for us to learn how to relax. ___(15)___ , taking a small break at least once a day might be a great idea.

First, sit in a cozy chair and relax as much as possible. Then, close your eyes and ___(16)___ the most peaceful scenery, such as a deep blue sea beside a huge land of green grass. Next, breathe in and out slowly and steadily, each time for a count of ten. Repeat the ___(17)___ several times, but remember to do it naturally and gracefully.

Finally, you will find such a break can ___(18)___ . Best of all, you can do it anywhere at any time without spending money or too much time.

⑮ _____

A. For example
B. On the contrary
C. All in all
D. In conclusion

⑯ _____

A. discuss
B. change
C. enjoy
D. imagine

⑰ _____

A. mistake
B. word
C. process
D. experiment

⑱ _____

A. make you feel tired
B. calm you and refresh you
C. hardly breathe
D. buy you some time

第三部分：閱讀理解

共 12 題，包括 4 個題組，每個題組含 1 至 2 篇短文，與數個相關的四選一的選擇題。請由試題冊上的選項中選出最適合的答案。

Questions 19–21

GOODBUY DEPARTMENT STORE
CUSTOMER SURVEY

1. Sex: ☐ male   ■ female
2. Age: ☐ 15–20   ☐ 21–29   ☐ 30–39   ■ 40–49   ☐ over 50
3. Length of trip from home to store:
   ☐ 1–10 mins   ☐ 11–20 mins   ■ over 20 mins
4. How do you get here?
   ☐ walk   ■ drive   ☐ take public transportation
5. How often do you shop here?
   ☐ once a year   ☐ once a month   ■ once a week
6. What products do you buy?
   ☐ cosmetics   ☐ shoes   ■ foods   ■ clothes   ■ household goods
   ☐ toys   ☐ bags

Chloe

_____ ⑲ Who might fill the form?

    A. A manager at the Goodbuy Department Store

    B. A clerk at the Goodbuy Department Store

    C. A doorman at the Goodbuy Department Store

    D. A customer at the Goodbuy Department Store

_____ ⑳ How long does it take the woman to get to the store?

    A. About 10 minutes

    B. 15 minutes

    C. More than 20 minutes

    D. Less than 5 minutes

_____ ㉑ What is **NOT** true about Ms. Chloe?

    A. She is in her forties now.

    B. She can't drive.

    C. She often goes shopping once a week.

    D. She seldom buys toys or bags at Goodbuy Department Store.

Questions 22–24

Many students from Taiwan go to New Zealand on a working holiday every year. They go to study English and experience life in New Zealand. New Zealand has wonderful scenery, which can be seen in *The Lord of the Rings* movies.

Students study with teachers from New Zealand, and talk with classmates from different countries in English. Students stay with local families so that they can practice daily English as well. English in New Zealand is a little different from that in the US. For example, students have fun learning new words like "cuppa" for a cup of tea or "spud" for potato. English is used in many countries and it is useful for students to understand how English works as an international language.

_____ ㉒ According to this article, why do students go to New Zealand?

    A. To learn English

    B. To shot films

    C. To have a cup of tea

    D. To enjoy the beautiful scenery

㉓ What does "cuppa" mean?

A.

B.

C.

D.

㉔ Which of the following is **NOT** true?

A. Students go to New Zealand to study Chinese.

B. *The Lord of the Rings* movies are shot in New Zealand.

C. Working holiday is a way to experience life in New Zealand.

D. English in New Zealand is slightly different from that in the US.

Questions 25–27

Dear Stanley,

    I am a regular customer of your restaurant, and I am writing this letter to tell you that one of your employees is very rude. I don't know her name, but she is a tall, thin girl with red hair.

    I went to your restaurant with my friend, Jenny, yesterday. She answered our questions about the meal in an impatient way. Her cellphone rang while she was taking our order. She said, "Hold on a minute, it is my boyfriend." Then she answered the phone. It was really unbelievable. I believed that we deserved more than this.

    Your restaurant serves the best beef Wellington in the city and I do love it. However, the service was horrible and so was the steak last night. I think I would never go to your restaurant again.

Sincerely,

Judy

＠ What is the purpose of this letter?

    A. To look for her missing coat

    B. To thank a nice waitress

    C. To compliment the chef on his cooking

    D. To complain about the bad service and food

＠ Who might be this rude waitress?

    A. Anna, a tall, slender blonde

    B. Claire, a tall, slim girl with red hair

    C. Sarah, a short, chubby girl with black hair

    D. Elsa, a young girl with long brown hair

＠ What made Judy and her friend angry?

    A. The waitress answered her phone call.

    B. The manager didn't reply her letter.

    C. The steak tasted as delicious as it used to be.

    D. The waiter messed up their orders.

Questions 28–30

According to a recent study, the number of deaths caused by heart disease, fatness, and diabetes has hit a record high. Being overweight does serious harm to a person's health. Therefore, the experts of health have warned governments all around the world to take this topic seriously. If we don't pay attention to it, we will have the first generation of kids living a shorter life than their parents.

In fact, it can be prevented simply by changing one's diet and lifestyle. Recently, the public is aware of the danger of being overweight. A growing number of people are now in the habit of exercising. There are also many videos about how to prepare a healthy meal on YouTube. Besides, more and more food companies are willing to provide customers with healthier menus.

＠ What is the purpose of this article?

    A. To ask overweight people to go on a diet

    B. To tell people that having heart disease is dangerous

    C. To prove how taking exercise helps lose a lot of weight

    D. To draw attention to the subject of being overweight

_____ ㉙ Which of the following is mentioned in this article?

    A. The risk factors for heart disease

    B. The skills of making YouTube videos

    C. Some useful ways of staying in shape

    D. Some workable solutions to reduce death rate

_____ ㉚ According to this article, which of the following is a good way to lose weight?

    A. Learning how to cook healthily online

    B. Seeing a doctor about fatness

    C. Developing the habit of eating out

    D. Watching videos about exercise

寫作能力測驗

第一部分：單句寫作

請將答案寫在答案欄中，如有文法、用字、拼字、標點符號、大小寫等錯誤，將予扣分。

第1～5題：句子改寫

請依題目之提示，將原句改寫成指定型式，並將改寫的句子**完整**地寫在答案欄中。注意：*每題均需寫出完整的句子，否則將予扣分。*

1 The dog barked at the postman.

The postman _____ .

2 Don't eat too much. You will gain weight.

If _____ .

3 Mom: Don't smoke anymore!

Dad: Oh! I'll stop it right now.

Dad will _____ .

4 Lisa's hobby is not the same as mine. (different)

My _____ .

5 Sue and Nancy are good students. Ann is better than them. (best)

Ann _____ .

第6～10題：句子合併

請依照題目指示，將兩句合併成一句，並將合併的句子**完整**地寫在答案欄中。注意：*每題均需寫出完整的句子，否則將予扣分。*

6 I'll lend you another book.

You return the book. (After...)

_____ .

7 Eric doesn't like music.

I don't like music, either. (...nor...)

_____ .

107

❽ Jack and Henry are my best friends.

Jack and Henry joined the school baseball team.

My _____ .

❾ The man sells beef.

The man makes a lot of money. (...by...)

_____ .

❿ Pandas eat bamboo.

Pandas eat fruit. (...either...or...)

_____ .

第 11～15 題：重組

　　請將題目中所有提示字詞整合成一有意義的句子，並將重組的句子**完整**地寫在答案欄中。*注意：每題均需寫出完整的句子。答案中必須使用所有提示字詞，且不能隨意增減字詞及標點符號，否則不予計分。*

⓫ The _____ .

was / knew / little girl / the candy / where

⓬ All _____ .

the concert / sold out / were / to / the tickets

⓭ It is _____ .

that / Dave / reading / doesn't love / a pity

⓮ How _____ ?

the pyramids / about / do you / much / know

⓯ I found _____ .

difficult / to sing / English / in / it

第二部分：段落寫作

題目：假設你是班級小記者，負責報導上週班級才藝競賽的成果，請根據以下圖片，寫一篇約 50 字的短文。**注意：未依提示作答者，將予扣分。**

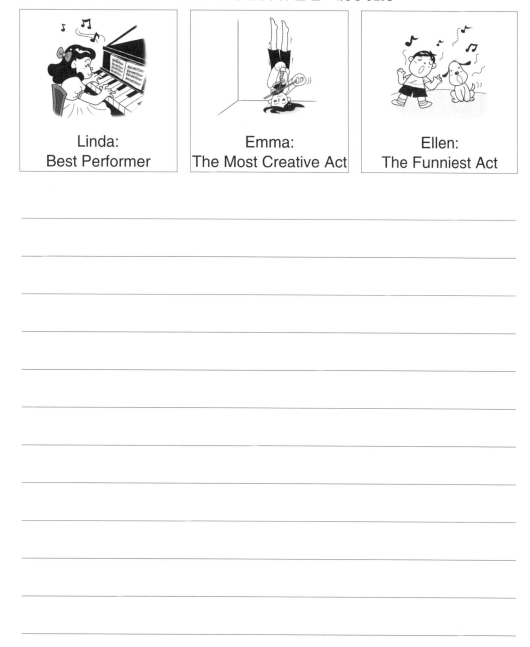

Linda:
Best Performer

Emma:
The Most Creative Act

Ellen:
The Funniest Act

口說能力測驗

🔊 Track 45

請在 15 秒內完成並唸出下列自我介紹的句子：

My seat number is （座位號碼後 5 碼）, and my test number is （考試號碼後 5 碼）.

第一部分：複誦 🔊 Track 46

共五題，經由音檔播出，每題播出兩次，兩次之間約有一至二秒的間隔。聽完兩次後，請立即複誦一次。

第二部分：朗讀句子與短文 🔊 Track 47

共有五個句子及一篇短文，請先利用一分鐘的時間閱讀句子與短文，然後在一分鐘內以正常的速度，清楚正確地朗讀一遍，閱讀時請不要發出聲音。

One: I know a lovely restaurant in town. We can go there for lunch.

Two: Can I get you anything to drink? Some coffee, or tea?

Three: Those phones are nice, but they are not within my budget.

Four: Well, since the shoes are on sale, I'll take a pair in black.

Five: Please make sure you're at the boarding gate 10 minutes before then.

Six: Eric Jones is from Australia, and he lives in Taiwan now. Although he has been to many countries in Europe and Asia, he likes Taiwan best. He has lived in Taipei for about three years. He especially loves Taiwanese food and culture. Eric is kind and outgoing, so he has made a lot of friends.

第三部分：回答問題 🔊 Track 48

共七題。經由音檔播出，每題播出兩次，兩次之間約有一至二秒的間隔。聽完兩次後，請立即回答，每題回答時間 15 秒，請在作答時間內盡量地表達。

請將下列自我介紹的句子再唸一遍：

My seat number is （座位號碼後 5 碼）, and my test number is （考試號碼後 5 碼）.

全民英檢初級模擬試題

TEST 7

聽力測驗

第一部分　看圖辨義

第二部分　問答

第三部分　簡短對話

第四部分　短文聽解

閱讀能力測驗

第一部分　詞彙

第二部分　段落填空

第三部分　閱讀理解

寫作能力測驗

第一部分　單句寫作

第二部分　段落寫作

口說能力測驗

第一部分　複誦

第二部分　朗讀句子與短文

第三部分　回答問題

聽力測驗

本測驗分四個部分，皆為單選題，共 30 題，作答時間約 20 分鐘。作答說明為中文，印在試題冊上並由音檔播出。

第一部分：看圖辨義 🔊 Track 49

共 5 題，每題請聽音檔播出題目和三個英語句子之後，選出與所看到的圖畫最相符的答案。每題只播出一遍。

A. Question 1

Answer ❶ : _____

B. Question 2

Answer ❷ : _____

C. Question 3

Answer ❸ : _____

D. Question 4

SLOW
DOWN
Beware of Children

Answer ❹ : _____

E. Question 5

Answer ❺ : _____

第二部分：問答 🔊 Track 50

共 10 題，每題請聽音檔播出的英語句子，再從試題冊上三個回答中，選出一個最適合的答案。每題只播出一遍。

❻ _____
A. It's about three kilometers.
B. I spend about $15.
C. It takes about an hour.

❼ _____
A. Why did you do that?
B. Why don't you put it back?
C. Why not put on your coat?

❽ _____
A. Just a few.
B. I don't eat meat.
C. A little, please.

❾ _____
A. I don't think so.
B. Taipei is crowded, too.
C. I've never been to America.

❿ _____
A. No, it's interesting.
B. It's too noisy for me.
C. It's great. I have a test on that day.

⓫ _____
A. My daughter didn't come with me.
B. Yes, we went to the restaurant together.
C. She went to the night market.

⓬ _____
A. No, I'm sorry, but you can't.
B. All right.
C. Yes, you do.

⓭ _____
A. I think the best place is Tainan.
B. Oh, I think the purple one is better on you.
C. Hamburgers are the best.

⓮ _____
A. I cannot finish the exercise alone.
B. After class, I often walk home.
C. Me too. So I come here more often.

⓯ _____
A. Yes. And I'm going to get her a jacket.
B. Well, I know she likes music.
C. No, but I'll invite Nancy's brother.

共 10 題，每題請聽音檔播出一段對話和一個相關的問題後，再從試題冊
上三個選項中，選出一個最適合的答案。每段對話和問題播出一遍。

⓰ _____
   A. As soon as possible.
   B. Three month ago.
   C. Next month.

⓱ _____
   A. After midnight.
   B. Before 10.
   C. At noon.

⓲ _____
   A. Save sea turtles.
   B. Major in ecology.
   C. Teach Mexicans.

⓳ _____
   A. Seeing a doctor.
   B. Sending the package.
   C. Buying stamps.

⓴ _____
   A. Wearing a seat belt.
   B. Driving slowly.
   C. Putting on glasses.

㉑ _____
   A. Three.
   B. Two.
   C. One.

㉒ _____
   A. A heart attack.
   B. High blood pressure.
   C. Overweight.

㉓ _____
   A. Crowded.
   B. Boring.
   C. Exciting.

㉔ _____
   A. He doesn't like Japanese.
   B. He can't pronounce Japanese
      words correctly.
   C. He can't get good grades on
      Japanese tests.

㉕ _____
   A. A restaurant.
   B. A travel agency.
   C. A hotel.

第四部分：短文聽解 🔊 Track 52

共 5 題，每題有三個圖片選項。請聽音檔播出的題目，並選出一個最適合的圖片。每題播出一遍。

㉖ _____

A.

B.

C.

㉗ _____

A.

B.

C.

㉘ _____

A.

B.

C.

㉙ _____

A. B. C.

㉚ _____

A. B. C.

閱讀能力測驗 ▌ 本測驗分三部分，全部都是單選題，共 30 題，作答時間 35 分鐘。

第一部分：詞彙

共 10 題，每個題目裡有一個空格。請從四個選項中選出一個最適合題意的字或詞作答。

_____ ❶ If you see a _____ in the sky, you may notice that it has seven colors.

       A. ballon   B. dancer   C. photo   D. rainbow

_____ ❷ I got a free book. In other words, I received it without having to make any

       _____.

       A. mistake   B. payment   C. practice   D. method

_____ ❸ You look so pretty in that dress. You can _____ it to my wedding.

       A. waste   B. wave   C. wear   D. wait

_____ ❹ Tony was fired last month. He can't _____ his rent anymore.

       A. send for   B. lend to   C. borrow from   D. pay for

_____ ❺ Jenny _____ to a new apartment. Her bedroom is even bigger than

       before.

       A. required   B. turned   C. moved   D. written

_____ ❻ Mr. Hunt was invited to _____ at the wedding.

       A. make a killing   B. make a speech

       C. make a living   D. make a bed

_____ ❼ In fact, I'm a bit worried. _____ my parents don't agree with that?

       A. How about   B. Why are   C. If only   D. What if

_____ ❽ Encouraged by his classmates, Ted won the contest and the NT$10,000

       _____.

       A. total   B. award   C. money   D. price

_____ ❾ The test was _____ and every student in my class got a high mark.

       A. a piece of cake   B. pie in the sky

       C. a white elephant   D. like a puzzle

_____ ❿ The bad guy killed the security guard when he _____ the bank.

       A. robbed   B. served   C. knocked   D. cheated

第二部分：段落填空

共 8 題，包括二個段落，每個段落各含四個空格。每格均有四個選項，請依文意選出最適合的答案。

Questions 11–14

In my free time, I often go to the hospital near my house and __(11)__ . Last Saturday, I was asked to __(12)__ Roy, a twelve-year-old boy. He was terribly ill and had been in the hospital for more than two years. When I entered his room, he smiled at me in an instant. We talked happily during my __(13)__ . He also shared his dream with me. __(14)__ he was ill, the brave boy dreamed of becoming a doctor one day. He said that he wanted to help other sick kids, just like what the doctors did here. I was touched and I told him I had faith in him.

⑪ _____
A. see a doctor there
B. visit my brother there
C. have an operation there
D. volunteer to help patients there

⑬ _____
A. travel
B. work
C. stay
D. speech

⑫ _____
A. take care of
B. look for
C. make fun of
D. catch up with

⑭ _____
A. But
B. Once
C. Although
D. Otherwise

Questions 15–18

My twin daughters, April and May, __(15)__ . April is shy. She will __(16)__ you first from far away before she plays with you. But once she is comfortable with you, she is very caring. Many times she shares her baby food with me __(17)__ lunch. On the other hand, May is outgoing and friendly. She laughs and plays with others easily. She is not shy __(18)__ .

These two little girls are growing so fast. They learn new things every day. They learn about their own likes and dislikes. I learn things about them every day, too.

⑮ _____
    A. are similar to each other
    B. have very different personalities
    C. are often shy of people they don't
       know
    D. have a lot of common interests

⑯ _____
    A. watch
    B. escape
    C. break
    D. tell

⑰ _____
    A. at
    B. by
    C. in
    D. for

⑱ _____
    A. in person
    B. in all
    C. at all
    D. in front

第三部分：閱讀理解

共 12 題，包括 4 個題組，每個題組含 1 至 2 篇短文，與數個相關的四選一的選擇題。請由試題冊上的選項中選出最適合的答案。

Questions 19–21

_____ ⑲ How many people are there in the Smiths?

      A. 11

      B. 12

      C. 14

      D. 15

_____ ⑳ Who is Julia Baxter?

      A. Paul's sister

      B. Anna's mother

      C. Sarah's daughter

      D. Tony's aunt

_____ ㉑ Which is true about the family tree?

      A. There are two generations in the Smith family.

      B. Steven has two children.

      C. Tony is Peter's uncle.

      D. Emily is Collin's cousin.

Questions 22–24

CLASSIFIEDS

Fashion Designer's Assistant
- Have a keen sense of fashion and know what styles are on trend.
- Advanced sewing skills are essential.

Call Miranda at 25XX-66XX

Babysitter Wanted
- Reliable, experienced, and friendly.
- Working on weekends from 2:00~10:00 pm.

Email to *lovelybaby@yahoo.com*

Green Coffee Is Hiring
- Funny, cute, and energetic.
- Be available at least 20 hours a week.
- No experience needed.

Contact with the manager Emma

Tour Guide
- Familiar with the old town area.
- Enjoy showing tourists around and good at public speaking.
- Working hours are flexible!

Mail to 168, Maple St., Spring City

_____ ㉒ Who would be interested in reading these classifieds?

A. Workers who hope to improve their technical skills.

B. Travelers who dream of traveling around the world.

C. People who are looking for a job.

D. Company owners who want to hire staff.

_____ ㉓ Andrea loves fashion and she always wears trendy clothes. What's important is that she made them by herself! What is the ideal job for her to do?

A. A babysitter

B. A tour guide

C. A coffee shop waitress

D. A fashion designer's assistant

_____ ㉔ Bruce loves those old buildings in his hometown. He would love to share the beauty of them to tourists. What should he do to apply for the job?

A. Call Miranda right away

B. Go to Green Coffee and find Emma

C. Sent his résumé to 168, Maple St., Spring City

D. Email his work experience to lovebaby@yahoo.com

Questions 25–27

Fanny Cooper has a dry throat. She felt dizzy and couldn't stop shaking. Her heart was almost beating its way out of her chest. She saw her face reflected in the window of the exam hall. All her prettiness was gone. She looked tired and pale with dark circles under her eyes. Her black hair looked greasy.

The exam paper for junior high school students was put on the desk in front of her. She called it "the test of life" because it will decide people's lives: who they will be, what jobs will they do, who will be their friends, who they will meet and marry. When she looked at the exam paper, numbers and letters moved around like disturbed ants. Even if she got them to stand still, she couldn't answer the questions. Her mind had gone blank.

㉕ According to this article, what was Fanny doing?

A.

B.

C.

D.

㉖ How did Fanny look?

A. She looked nervous.

B. She looked pretty.

C. She looked angry.

D. She looked happy.

㉗ What can we infer about Fanny?

A. There were many ants on her test paper.

B. She was confident about the test.

C. She is a senior high school student.

D. She might do badly on the test.

Questions 28–30

Blue whales are the largest animals which are ever known to have lived on Earth. However, it is next to impossible for you to see one in person because it's too huge to keep in a zoo. An adult blue whale is up to 200 tons in weight. Blue whales sing to share information with each other. They have one of the loudest calls in the animal kingdom. Their sounds are louder than an aircraft noise and can be heard from 800 kilometers away. When blue whales come up for fresh air, they blow out the air they have held in their lungs and then take new air. The air they blow out is warm. When it hits cooler air, it turns to steam which is called the whale's spout.

_____ ❷❽ Which of the following is the best title for this article?

    A. Blue Whales—The Largest Animals in History

    B. How Blue Whales Talk with Each Other

    C. The Best Time and Place to Watch Blue Whales

    D. Some Amazing Facts About Blue Whales

_____ ❷❾ What information about blue whales is **NOT** provided in this article?

    A. How much they weigh

    B. How they find their mates

    C. How they share information

    D. How they breathe

_____ ❸❶ According to this article, which of the following about blue whales is true?

    A. They breathe with lungs.

    B. They shout to talk with each other.

    C. The whale's spout is in the form of ice.

    D. A baby blue whale weighs more than 200 tons.

寫作能力測驗 ▌

第一部分：單句寫作

請將答案寫在答案欄中，如有文法、用字、拼字、標點符號、大小寫等錯誤，將予扣分。

第 1～5 題：句子改寫

請依題目之提示，將原句改寫成指定型式，並將改寫的句子**完整**地寫在答案欄中。*注意：每題均需寫出完整的句子，否則將予扣分。*

❶ There are seven days in a week.

How many _____?

❷ Lisa is eight years old.

Lisa _____ girl.

❸ It was cold outside, so I put on a heavy coat.

Because _____.

❹ The dog is lying under the table.

It is _____.

❺ Simon is a very good science teacher.

Simon teaches _____.

第 6～10 題：句子合併

請依照題目指示，將兩句合併成一句，並將合併的句子**完整**地寫在答案欄中。*注意：每題均需寫出完整的句子，否則將予扣分。*

❻ It was not because of the place.

It was because of the people. (...but...)

_____.

❼ Tanya is going to be a lawyer.

This is her ambition.

Tanya's _____.

❽ I saw Peter in the café.

Peter was chatting with a girl in the café.

I saw Peter _____.

❾ Albert didn't say a word.

Albert left the classroom. (...without...)

_____ .

❿ Dave was sweeping the floor.

The teacher made Dave do it.

The teacher _____ .

第 11～15 題：重組

　　請將題目中所有提示字詞整合成一有意義的句子，並將重組的句子**完整**地寫在答案欄中。**注意：*每題均需寫出完整的句子。答案中必須使用所有提示字詞，且不能隨意增減字詞及標點符號，否則不予計分。***

⓫ What _____ ?

do you / to watch / kind of / like / movies

⓬ My _____

decided / smoking / has / to quit / brother

⓭ You _____ .

have to / to me / say / don't / sorry

⓮ There _____ .

the river / many joggers / are / running / along

⓯ The weather _____ .

in Taipei / in Tainan / that / is colder / than

126

第二部分：段落寫作

題目：下面兩張照片分別為 Kevin 在國中與大學時期的照片 ，第三張是他未來的夢想，請根據以下圖片寫一篇約 50 字的短文介紹 Kevin。**注意：未依提示作答者，將予扣分。**

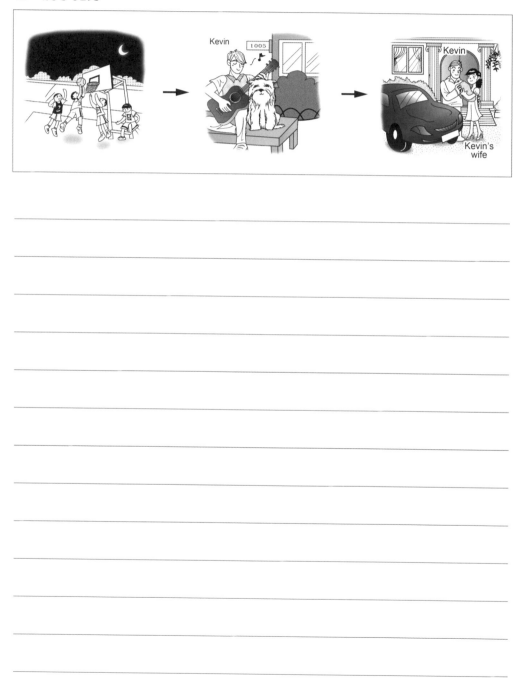

_____

_____

_____

_____

_____

_____

_____

_____

_____

_____

_____

_____

_____

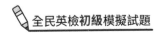

 Track 53

請在 15 秒內完成並唸出下列自我介紹的句子：

My seat number is （座位號碼後 5 碼）, and my test number is （考試號碼後 5 碼）.

第一部分：複誦 🔊 Track 54

共五題，經由音檔播出，每題播出兩次，兩次之間約有一至二秒的間隔。聽完兩次後，請立即複誦一次。

第二部分：朗讀句子與短文 🔊 Track 55

共有五個句子及一篇短文，請先利用一分鐘的時間閱讀句子與短文，然後在一分鐘內以正常的速度，清楚正確地朗讀一遍，閱讀時請不要發出聲音。

One: You study all the time! You should take a break.

Two: Families usually get together to celebrate Chinese New Year.

Three: Please wait a moment when I check the list.

Four: Excuse me. I have a problem with my computer.

Five: I think he'll be very successful.

Six: Last year, I met Paul at the gym, and it changed my life. I told Paul that lifting weights was something that I had always wanted to try. Therefore, he helped me start an exercise program. After that, I went to gym every day. Now I become stronger and happier than ever.

第三部分：回答問題 🔊 Track 56

共七題。經由音檔播出，每題播出兩次，兩次之間約有一至二秒的間隔。聽完兩次後，請立即回答，每題回答時間 15 秒，請在作答時間內盡量地表達。

請將下列自我介紹的句子再唸一遍：

My seat number is （座位號碼後 5 碼）, and my test number is （考試號碼後 5 碼）.

全民英檢初級模擬試題

TEST 8

聽力測驗
第一部分　看圖辨義
第二部分　問答
第三部分　簡短對話
第四部分　短文聽解

閱讀能力測驗
第一部分　詞彙
第二部分　段落填空
第三部分　閱讀理解

寫作能力測驗
第一部分　單句寫作
第二部分　段落寫作

口說能力測驗
第一部分　複誦
第二部分　朗讀句子與短文
第三部分　回答問題

聽力測驗 ┃ 本測驗分四個部分,皆為單選題,共 30 題,作答時間約 20 分鐘。作答說明為中文,印在試題冊上並由音檔播出。

第一部分:看圖辨義 🔊 Track 57

共 5 題,每題請聽音檔播出題目和三個英語句子之後,選出與所看到的圖畫最相符的答案。每題只播出一遍。

A. Question 1

Answer ❶ : _____

B. Questions 2 and 3

Answer ❷ : _____　❸ : _____

C. Question 4

2021/08/08   Train 136   one-way ticket

Taipei → Taichung
11:20   **12:15**

8 CAR 4A   NT$700   Credit Card
10-5-66-0-178-0018   Adult

Answer ❹ : _____

D. Question 5

Answer ❺ : _____

第二部分：問答 🔊 Track 58

共 10 題，每題請聽音檔播出的英語句子，再從試題冊上三個回答中，選出一個最適合的答案。每題只播出一遍。

⑥ _____
A. No, that's all.
B. OK. Anything else?
C. Oh, yes. I'd like some pasta.

⑦ _____
A. Yes, of course.
B. No. Not at all.
C. Actually, I'm a bit cold.

⑧ _____
A. I like classical music too.
B. I can't stand it. It's too noisy.
C. I would rather dine out.

⑨ _____
A. They were running for the train.
B. He was hanging out at the mall.
C. Did you? What was he doing there?

⑩ _____
A. Oh, cut my finger when I was chooping carrots.
B. You should be more careful.
C. Did you go to the doctor yet?

⑪ _____
A. I met Tom in the street.
B. I should get my passport and visa first.
C. I'm going to New Zealand with my family.

⑫ _____
A. I'm not sure. I might take chemistry.
B. No. He might take physics.
C. For me, medicine is the best choice for my cousin.

⑬ _____
A. I clean up rooms every day.
B. Not really. It's a part-time job.
C. It's fun to be with you.

⑭ _____
A. I cook dinner for my family.
B. What's your favorite dish to cook?
C. Yes, I have meeting on that day.

⑮ _____
A. I can't believe she stole it from the store.
B. Yes, you can say that again.
C. Do you know that woman in a fur hat?

共 10 題，每題請聽音檔播出一段對話和一個相關的問題後，再從試題冊
上三個選項中，選出一個最適合的答案。每段對話和問題播出一遍。

⑯ _____
A. On a Monday or Tuesday.
B. In the middle of the week.
C. On a Saturday or Sunday.

⑰ _____
A. Music genres.
B. A musician's biography.
C. Their favorite novelists.

⑱ _____
A. He was late for school.
B. He didn't prepare well.
C. He missed his mom.

⑲ _____
A. Spend all of them.
B. Give it to the police.
C. Put it in the bank.

⑳ _____
A. Jazz.
B. Heavy metal.
C. R&B.

㉑ _____
A. Your confidence.
B. Your interest.
C. The population.

㉒ _____
A. The man's.
B. The woman's.
C. A girl named Cindy.

㉓ _____
A. Exercising.
B. He is late for school.
C. Chasing a thief.

㉔ _____
A. Cool stuff.
B. A nice hat.
C. Volleyball.

㉕ _____
A. A place to travel.
B. A famous star.
C. Sport.

第四部分：短文聽解 🔊 Track 60

共 5 題，每題有三個圖片選項。請聽音檔播出的題目，並選出一個最適合的圖片。每題播出一遍。

26 _____

A. B. C.

27 _____

A. B. C.

28 _____

A. B. C.

29 _____

A.

B.

C.

30 _____

A.

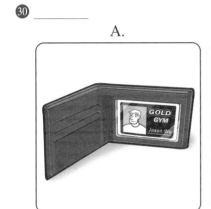

B.

C.

閱讀能力測驗 | 本測驗分三部分，全部都是單選題，共 30 題，作答時間 35 分鐘。

第一部分：詞彙

共 10 題，每個題目裡有一個空格。請從四個選項中選出一個最適合題意的字或詞作答。

_____ ❶ Are you afraid that I might _____ the exam?

       A. fail   B. fall   C. mail   D. meet

_____ ❷ Keep working hard _____ you will succeed at last.

       A. or   B. nor   C. before   D. and

_____ ❸ Let him sleep in. Don't wake him up. He _____ late last night.

       A. shut up   B. stayed up   C. showed up   D. got up

_____ ❹ All my classmates are busy making a plan for _____ the school trip.

       A. discussing   B. planting   C. delivering   D. praising

_____ ❺ Parents have a _____ to protect their children.

       A. habit   B. policy   C. freedom   D. duty

_____ ❻ Anna's shoes are not as new as mine. She has _____ them for a long time.

       A. woke   B. wanted   C. wrote   D. worn

_____ ❼ I am trying hard to finish the report because it's _____ this week.

       A. full   B. due   C. daily   D. late

_____ ❽ My boss _____ me to send the customer an email right away.

       A. advised   B. answered   C. employed   D. doubted

_____ ❾ Be careful! The new knife is as _____ as a razor. It might hurt you.

       A. selfish   B. short   C. sharp   D. strong

_____ ❿ Few people want to make friends with a person who likes to _____ his expensive things.

       A. show off   B. run into   C. turn down   D. look after

第二部分：段落填空

共 8 題，包括二個段落，每個段落各含四個空格。每格均有四個選項，請依文意選出最適合的答案。

Questions 11–14

In San Francisco, people use public transportation all the time. There is a subway station outside my home. I ride the subway all ___(11)___ the city. It's really convenient. I take the bus, too. There are many bus stops near my apartment. And sometimes I walk. I get around ___(12)___ foot to places nearby.

However, in California, public transportation isn't ___(13)___ convenient. When I go there, I drive my car a lot. Many other people drive their cars, too. There is a lot of traffic so that people can't get to places very fast.

Actually, ___(14)___. Some people take a plane or a train to a faraway city. Some people take a taxi to a restaurant or a store. Still others take a boat or a ship. They can always get to where they want to go.

⑪ _____
A. about
B. of
C. over
D. above

⑫ _____
A. on
B. by
C. with
D. from

⑬ _____
A. as
B. much
C. all
D. that

⑭ _____
A. there are many other kinds of transportation
B. no one likes to take public transportation
C. it's difficult to take public transportation
D. there's no difference between train and taxi

Questions 15–18

Taiwan has many beautiful scenic places, and Taroko National Park is one of ___(15)___. Taroko National Park ___(16)___ the eastern part of Taiwan. It attracts many tourists from around the world to come to here each year. When they get this place, they will be ___(17)___ by the towering cliffs, deep marble canyons, and crystal-clear waterfalls here. Besides, Taroko National Park is ___(18)___. For example, visitors can find unique weaving skills and various traditional handicrafts here. As a natural area with aboriginal traditions, Taroko National Park is well worth a visit.

⑮ _____
    A. they
    B. them
    C. it
    D. themselves

⑰ _____
    A. irritated
    B. praised
    C. annoyed
    D. fascinated

⑯ _____
    A. has been
    B. lies in
    C. is placed under
    D. at

⑱ _____
    A. also famous for its aboriginal culture
    B. full of foreign culture
    C. also a nice place to live
    D. difficult for people to reach

第三部分：閱讀理解

共 12 題，包括 4 個題組，每個題組含 1 至 2 篇短文，與數個相關的四選一的選擇題。請由試題冊上的選項中選出最適合的答案。

Questions 19–21

RizBeta

Best Free Comparison Shopping Site
➲ **FIND** your best deals from all of the top-rated stores.
➲ **COMPARE** your products/prices quickly.
➲ **READ** product reviews instantly.
➲ **CHOOSE** your right product at the right price!

Come and Shop Smarter at www.RizBeta.com

_____ ⑲ When can people probably find this ad?
    A. While visiting to a museum
    B. When surfing the Internet

C. When watching a movie

D. After paying the check

_____ **⑳** What may **NOT** be found in this site?

A. Products

B. Prices

C. Reviews

D. Locations

_____ **㉑** Which is true about the site?

A. People can shop at RizBeta freely.

B. RizBeta is a good site for shoppers to check the prices of products.

C. Customers can't read the product reviews after they buy.

D. RizBeta sells top-rated products only.

Questions 22–24

Below is Jason's diary.

Feb. 3rd

Dear diary,

    I read the fourth part of *The Dog that Plays Soccer* today. Jimmy's mother called the news station. They came and took photos of "Spot," the dog that could play soccer. Lots of people saw the news on TV. Then they came to Jimmy's house to see Spot and play soccer with it. However, the next morning when Jimmy woke up, he couldn't find Spot anywhere. To make things worse, Jimmy was hit by a car when he was searching for Spot on the streets. Doctors said that Jimmy needed immediate surgery.

    The last part of the story will be published in July. I cannot wait to see how it ends and I hope it has a happy ending.

_____ ㉒ Which of the following is the best time for Jimmy to have surgery?

A. After he finds Spot.

B. When the doctors are available.

C. As soon as possible.

D. Before people know that he was hit by a car.

_____ ㉓ How long will Jason wait before he reads the last part of the story?

A. 5 days

B. July

C. February 3rd

D. About 5 months

_____ ㉔ What might happen to Spot?

A.

B.

C.

D.

Questions 25–27

It's time to say thank you to your teachers. September 28 is Teacher's Day. It's also Confucius' birthday. Confucius was a great teacher a long time ago. He once said, "Teach all students who want to learn." For students are not all the same. Some are rich, while some are poor; some like art and some like science. Confucius also said teachers should understand their students, which is the best way for students to learn quickly and easily.

Every year on September 28, big celebrations will be held at Confucius Temples all over Taiwan in honor of Confucius. Many people will come to these temples to **participate in** the ceremony and show their respect to Confucius.

_____ ㉕ Who is Confucius?

    A. A great artist

    B. A great scientist

    C. A great teacher

    D. A great student

_____ ㉖ Which of the following is said by Confucius?

    A. Teach all students who want to learn.

    B. Teach students who like science.

    C. Teach smart students.

    D. Teachers don't have to understand their students.

_____ ㉗ What does "**participate in**" in the last paragraph most likely refer to?

    A. deal with

    B. hold on

    C. observe

    D. take part in

Questions 28–30

Due to the COVID-19 restriction, Terry and Lisa are going to postpone their wedding. Below is the announcement to their guests.

WEDDING
POSTPONED

HOSTED BY TERRY & LISA

We can't imagine our wedding without
our friends and family there,
so we're rescheduling our wedding to
a time when we can all party safely.
Please save our new date:
Saturday June 23rd, 2021
Thanks for your understanding.
Please RSVP as soon as possible by e-mail.
lisa1205@umail.com
Be safe and be well.

_____ ㉘ Which of the following statement is true?

    A. People can eat outside.

    B. People can attend a funeral.

    C. People should maintain social distancing.

    D. Terry and Lisa are going to cancel their wedding.

_____ ㉙ Who is Terry?

    A. Lisa's father

    B. Lisa's brother

    C. Lisa's fiancé

    D. Lisa's son

_____ ㉚ How to answer this invitation?

    A. Via phone call

    B. Via e-mail

    C. Via fax

    D. Via message

寫作能力測驗 ▌

第一部分：單句寫作

請將答案寫在答案欄中，如有文法、用字、拼字、標點符號、大小寫等錯誤，將予扣分。

第 1～5 題：句子改寫

請依題目之提示，將原句改寫成指定型式，並將改寫的句子**完整**地寫在答案欄中。*注意：每題均需寫出完整的句子，否則將予扣分。*

❶ It cost her NT$12,500 to buy this camera.

She _____ .

❷ The novel interested many children.

Many children _____ .

❸ If we have no money, we can't go anywhere.

Without _____ .

❹ The car accident was terrible!

How _____ !

❺ Mrs. Smith was talking to Danny in the hall.

Whom _____ ?

第 6～10 題：句子合併

請依照題目指示，將兩句合併成一句，並將合併的句子**完整**地寫在答案欄中。*注意：每題均需寫出完整的句子，否則將予扣分。*

❻ I was asked to do that.

I answered those questions in ten minutes.

_____ .

❼ You did me a big favor.

You are nice.

It is _____ .

❽ The man is old.

The man cannot walk fast. (...too...to...)

_____ .

143

❾ Children don't like to read.

Adults don't like to read. (Neither...nor...)

_____.

❿ Dad is watching TV.

Mom is cleaning the living room.

While Dad _____.

第 11～15 題：重組

請將題目中所有提示字詞整合成一有意義的句子，並將重組的句子**完整**地寫在答案欄中。*注意：每題均需寫出完整的句子。答案中必須使用所有提示字詞，且不能隨意增減字詞及標點符號，否則不予計分。*

⓫ I'm _____.

seeing you / soon / to / looking / forward

⓬ The boy _____.

the ceiling / enough / tall / to touch / is

⓭ Ted couldn't _____.

got up / late / because / catch / he / the bus

⓮ What _____?

order / I / do / the juice / you / think of

⓯ It is _____.

the medicine / necessary / to take / him / for

第二部分：段落寫作

題目：請根據以下的圖片寫一篇 50 字的短文，描述小狗所經歷的事件，並提供合理的解釋與結局。**注意：未依提示作答者，將予扣分。**

口說能力測驗

🔊 Track 61

請在 15 秒內完成並唸出下列自我介紹的句子：

My seat number is （座位號碼後 5 碼）, and my test number is （考試號碼後 5 碼）.

第一部分：複誦 🔊 Track 62

共五題，經由音檔播出，每題播出兩次，兩次之間約有一至二秒的間隔。聽完兩次後，請立即複誦一次。

第二部分：朗讀句子與短文 🔊 Track 63

共有五個句子及一篇短文，請先利用一分鐘的時間閱讀句子與短文，然後在一分鐘內以正常的速度，清楚正確地朗讀一遍，閱讀時請不要發出聲音。

One:　He has gone to the market to buy some fruit.

Two:　These rocks have helped us learn more about Mars.

Three:　Go straight and turn right at the corner. It's next to the bank.

Four:　I don't really like going to the concert or listening to pop music.

Five:　More than 3,000 people died, and almost 100,000 buildings fell down.

Six:　A good way to pass an exam is to work hard every day. You may fail the exam if you work hard only a few days before the exam. Take English for example. Try to read stories in English and talk in English whenever you can. And never give up.

第三部分：回答問題 🔊 Track 64

共七題。經由音檔播出，每題播出兩次，兩次之間約有一至二秒的間隔。聽完兩次後，請立即回答，每題回答時間 15 秒，請在作答時間內盡量地表達。

請將下列自我介紹的句子再唸一遍：

My seat number is （座位號碼後 5 碼）, and my test number is （考試號碼後 5 碼）.

全民英檢初級模擬試題

TEST 9

聽力測驗
第一部分　看圖辨義

第二部分　問答

第三部分　簡短對話

第四部分　短文聽解

閱讀能力測驗
第一部分　詞彙

第二部分　段落填空

第三部分　閱讀理解

寫作能力測驗
第一部分　單句寫作

第二部分　段落寫作

口說能力測驗
第一部分　複誦

第二部分　朗讀句子與短文

第三部分　回答問題

聽力測驗

本測驗分四個部分，皆為單選題，共 30 題，作答時間約 20 分鐘。作答說明為中文，印在試題冊上並由音檔播出。

第一部分：看圖辨義 🔊 Track 65

共 5 題，每題請聽音檔播出題目和三個英語句子之後，選出與所看到的圖畫最相符的答案。每題只播出一遍。

A. Question 1

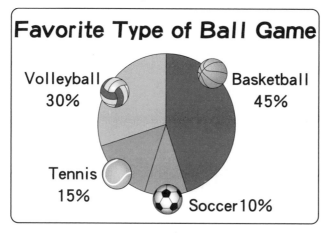

Answer ❶ : _____

B. Question 2

Answer ❷ : _____

C. Question 3

UK from only $4000
Save up to 20%
BOOK NOW

WWW.IFLY.COM

Answer ❸ : _____

D. Questions 4 and 5

Answer ❹ : _____ ❺ : _____

第二部分：問答 🔊 Track 66

共 10 題，每題請聽音檔播出的英語句子，再從試題冊上三個回答中，選出一個最適合的答案。每題只播出一遍。

6 _____
A. Yes, it's near the toilet.
B. Yes, I like the window seat.
C. Yes, there's more space.

7 _____
A. It's about 3 feet by 4 feet.
B. I bought it for NT$300.
C. It took me three hours to fix it.

8 _____
A. Yes, I was born into a poor family.
B. No, I was born in Hualien, Taiwan.
C. No, I was an only child.

9 _____
A. Yes, they are always so busy.
B. No, they don't match.
C. OK, I'll let you know.

10 _____
A. Yes, I can't wait for it to be over.
B. Yes, I can't wait to be there with you.
C. Yes, I'm worried that I won't do it well.

11 _____
A. I will remember you.
B. Yes, I did a great job.
C. Thanks for reminding me.

12 _____
A. No way.
B. Oh, no. We're late again.
C. Oh, you're right—the camera.

13 _____
A. I'll do it right now.
B. Oh, that's so nice of you.
C. Don't do that again, OK?

14 _____
A. The people there are friendly.
B. I can only stay there for a day.
C. My smartphone was stolen when I visited there.

15 _____
A. OK, perhaps next time.
B. I can't. Sorry.
C. No, I think that's all.

共 10 題，每題請聽音檔播出一段對話和一個相關的問題後，再從試題冊
上三個選項中，選出一個最適合的答案。每段對話和問題播出一遍。

⑯ _____
　A. Memorize the play script.
　B. Buy the tickets.
　C. Practice singing.

⑰ _____
　A. Cute.
　B. Scary.
　C. Clever.

⑱ _____
　A. It rained heavily.
　B. It snowed all day long.
　C. It was terribly hot.

⑲ _____
　A. Her bicycle.
　B. A rented car.
　C. The subway.

⑳ _____
　A. An engineer.
　B. A scientist.
　C. A teacher.

㉑ _____
　A. Before she does her homework.
　B. Early in the morning.
　C. At seven o'clock.

㉒ _____
　A. He will take the train.
　B. He can't go to school.
　C. He has to wait for the next one.

㉓ _____
　A. New Street.
　B. Park Street.
　C. Main Street.

㉔ _____
　A. Visiting cousins.
　B. Learning how to ride a horse.
　C. On Friday.

㉕ _____
　A. Relax.
　B. Study.
　C. Listen to music.

TEST ⑨

Listening

第四部分：短文聽解 🔊 Track 68

共 5 題，每題有三個圖片選項。請聽音檔播出的題目，並選出一個最適合的圖片。每題播出一遍。

㉖ _____

A.

B.

C.

㉗ _____

A.

B.

C.

㉘ _____

A.

B.

29

| | A. | B. | C. |

30

| | A. | B. | C. |

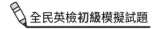

閱讀能力測驗 ▌本測驗分三部分，全部都是單選題，共 30 題，作答時間 35 分鐘。

第一部分：詞彙

共 10 題，每個題目裡有一個空格。請從四個選項中選出一個最適合題意的字或詞作答。

_____ ❶ We are looking _____ to working with you on this project.

　　A. forward　　　B. backward　　　C. toward　　　D. upward

_____ ❷ Don't look down on the boy. He may become a(n) _____ in the future.

　　A. nobody　　　B. anybody　　　C. somebody　　D. everybody

_____ ❸ The longer I live _____, the more I get used to being away from home.

　　A. abroad　　　B. ahead　　　C. aloud　　　D. alike

_____ ❹ My mom stopped me from going on a diet since I was already far too _____.

　　A. sleepy　　　B. skinny　　　C. shy　　　D. silly

_____ ❺ How much you get _____ how much effort you put into it.

　　A. results in　　B. focuses on　　C. depends on　　D. turns out

_____ ❻ I can't make up my mind _____ to quit my job or not.

　　A. if　　　　　B. how　　　　C. whether　　　D. in order

_____ ❼ Frankly _____, most of us don't speak English in our classroom.

　　A. speaking　　B. telling　　C. saying　　　D. talking

_____ ❽ The picture book is designed _____ for children. Most words in it are easy.

　　A. patiently　　B. negatively　　C. partly　　　D. primarily

_____ ❾ _____ losing my house keys this morning, I've had a great day.

　　A. Rather than　　B. Other than　　C. More than　　D. Less than

_____ ❿ We need to _____ out why she lied to us.

　　A. turn　　　　B. sell　　　　C. put　　　　D. figure

第二部分：段落填空

共 8 題，包括二個段落，每個段落各含四個空格。每格均有四個選項，請依文意選出最適合的答案。

Questions 11–14

Last Saturday, at about 5 o'clock in the morning, my family and I were woken up __(11)__ the ring of the fire alarm. We were surprised to see __(12)__ everywhere. Dad told us to stay calm, and Mom told us to lower __(13)__ to the ground. It was hard to see clearly in the dark, but we were very lucky to be able to get to the door and get out quickly.

We lost everything in the house. I was very upset. But Mom and Dad said that thank God nobody was hurt in the fire. __(14)__ Above all, I did not lose the most precious in my life—my beloved family.

⓫ _____
- A. by
- B. at
- C. with
- D. to

⓬ _____
- A. money
- B. water
- C. smoke
- D. furniture

⓭ _____
- A. herself
- B. ourselves
- C. himself
- D. themselves

⓮ _____
- A. I lost my parents.
- B. We spent a week in the hospital.
- C. Their conclusion was wrong.
- D. I guess they were right.

Questions 15–18

If tomorrow were the end of the world, I would try to be brave and spend the day with my family. In the morning, I would __(15)__ early and go to the nearby market with my mom. On our way there, we would walk hand __(16)__ hand and talk about what our lunch would be. In the market, I would help my mom __(17)__ her bags with our favorite food inside. __(18)__, I would set the table. After having a big meal, I would help my dad feed Lucky, our pet cat. I would give Lucky a bath and play with it for a while. During our last dinner, I would give each of my family members a big hug, and said, "I love you all. Good night!"

⑮ _____
A. turn up
B. close up
C. stand up
D. get up

⑯ _____
A. to
B. by
C. in
D. around

⑰ _____
A. carrying
B. in carrying
C. carry
D. to carry out

⑱ _____
A. Before going to the market
B. Then as the dishes were ready
C. After finishing our lunch
D. At the end of the world

第三部分：閱讀理解

共 12 題，包括 4 個題組，每個題組含 1 至 2 篇短文，與數個相關的四選一的選擇題。請由試題冊上的選項中選出最適合的答案。

Questions 19–21

PARADISE HOTEL GUEST REGISTRATION CARD		
Name *Anna Spencer Holmes*	Title *Ms.*	Room# *816*
Home Address *#1546, Mason St., Solo City*	Cost of Room *$85*　　　per night	
Nationality *Korea*	Room Type *Single*	
Phone No. *(054)288-7630*	Special Requirement *Non-smoking*	
Arrival time *25/07/21*	Departure time *29/07/21*	Payment Method □ Cash □ Check ■ Credit card □ Mobile payment
Signature 　　　　　　*Anna Holmes*		

_____ ⑲ How many nights will Anna spend at Paradise Hotel?

   A. 3   B. 4

   C. 5   D. 6

_____ ㉑ How will Anna pay her bill?

A.

B.

C.

D.

_____ ㉑ Which is **NOT** true about the guest?

A. She doesn't like to smoke.

B. She travels alone this time.

C. She is a Korean.

D. She has to pay $105 per night.

Questions 22–24

From: Meredith Shepherd

To: Amelia Grey

Amelia,

I am sorry I didn't reply to your e-mail earlier. I had a problem with my e-mail system for over a week, and I couldn't get any e-mails. Thank you for inviting me to go to Japan with you. And yes, I would love to go with you. Please tell me more about the travel plans, so I can adjust my work schedule. By the way, I will go on a business trip to Korea tomorrow. You can call me or e-mail me. Oh, I can't wait to travel with you again!

Meredith

_____ ㉒ Why didn't Meredith respond to Amelia's e-mail quickly?

    A. Her computer was broken.

    B. There was a problem with her e-mail system.

    C. She was on a business trip to Korea.

    D. She forgot the password.

_____ ㉓ What's Meredith's purpose of writing this letter?

    A. To promise Amelia that she will hand her design in on time

    B. To check her work schedule with Amelia

    C. To book a ticket to Japan

    D. To tell Amelia that she would love to go to Japan with her

_____ ㉔ What will Amelia most probably do after she gets the e-mail?

    A. She will send Meredith the travel plans.

    B. She will take several days off from work.

    C. She will go to Korea with Meredith.

    D. She will go on a business trip.

Questions 25–27

    When do you usually go shopping in a supermarket? Do you always buy a lot of things that you really don't need when you leave the supermarket? Or do you think buying things in a supermarket is a waste of time? Here are some tips that can help you solve these problems.

· Don't bring too much money with you. Otherwise you will end up buying too many unnecessary things.

· Make a list of all the items you want to buy. Do not buy anything that is not on your list.

· Use coupon and you can buy some items at a discount.

· Don't hang out at supermarkets. It makes you buy more things and cost you more money.

· Go to a supermarket on weekdays, so you will not waste time waiting in lines for checking out.

㉕ What is the main idea of this article?

    A. To teach people how to save their money and time.

    B. Never buy things in a supermarket.

    C. Don't be rude to the cashier in a supermarket.

    D. It is important to make ends meet.

㉖ According to the article, what day is the best day to go to a supermarket?

    A. Sunday

    B. Saturday

    C. Tuesday

    D. None of the above

㉗ Which of the following tips is **NOT** offered by the author?

    A. The more you buy the more you save

    B. Buy things that are on your shopping list

    C. Go to a supermarket with a limited budget

    D. A supermarket is not a good place to kill time

Questions 28–30

It's quite common to see brothers and sisters competing with each other. It isn't always a bad thing—one of the advantages is that it will keep people working hard. When someone beats you, it's easy to feel upset. But if it's your brother or sister who gets an award, you might feel a little jealous of his or her success. Why couldn't it be you that those great things happened to? Although you love your brothers and sisters, it's normal to be jealous, and you could be forgiven for that. The best way to get rid of the feelings of jealousy is not to battle against each other and have confidence in yourself. Maybe your sister won praise from teachers, but you might make an excellent job of doing a painting next week.

㉘ What is the author's attitude toward fights among brothers and sisters?

    A. Negative

    B. Positive

    C. Doubtful

    D. Amazed

_____ ㉙ What is the advantage of competition between brothers and sisters?

A. Making people feel upset

B. Keeping people feeling jealous

C. Pushing people to make an effort

D. Making it easy for people to forgive

_____ ㉚ According to this article, what might be the best way to deal with jealousy?

A. Fighting with others

B. Drawing a great painting

C. Praising others more frequently

D. Being confident of oneself

寫作能力測驗

第一部分：單句寫作

請將答案寫在答案欄中，如有文法、用字、拼字、標點符號、大小寫等錯誤，將予扣分。

第 1～5 題：句子改寫

請依題目之提示，將原句改寫成指定型式，並將改寫的句子**完整**地寫在答案欄中。**注意：*每題均需寫出完整的句子，否則將予扣分。***

1 I lent him three comic books.

He _____ .

2 Mary has no time at all. (...not...)

Mary _____ .

3 Sam was too sick to take a shower. (...so...that...)

Sam _____ .

4 Amy is the most beautiful girl in class.

No other girls _____ .

5 I don't like Eric, but I still support him.

Though _____ .

第 6～10 題：句子合併

請依照題目指示，將兩句合併成一句，並將合併的句子**完整**地寫在答案欄中。**注意：*每題均需寫出完整的句子，否則將予扣分。***

6 Lucy is 160 cm in height.

Lisa is 165 cm in height. (Lisa...than...)

_____ .

7 The phone rings.

I answer the phone. (If...)

_____ .

8 Mr. White is going to stop working next month.

Mr. White taught us math. (...who...)

_____ .

⑨ You study hard.

You fail the exams. (..., or...)

_____.

⑩ John was a hero.

No one believed that.

_____.

第 11～15 題：重組

　　請將題目中所有提示字詞整合成一有意義的句子，並將重組的句子**完整**地寫在答案欄中。**注意：*每題均需寫出完整的句子。答案中必須使用所有提示字詞，且不能隨意增減字詞及標點符號，否則不予計分。***

⑪ I _____.

saw / red bike / stealing / the / the man

⑫ Seldom _____.

wash / before dinner / he / his hands / did

⑬ Jane _____.

ran / with / the music classroom / her friends / into

⑭ My _____.

my birthday gift / gave / brother / me / as / a guitar

⑮ The _____.

in the restaurant / to smoke / not / asked us / waiter

第二部分：段落寫作

題目：上週你和家人度過了颱風天，請根據以下圖片寫一篇約 50 字的短文，描述你所遭遇到的事件。**注意：未依提示作答者，將予扣分。**

_____

_____

_____

_____

_____

_____

_____

_____

_____

_____

_____

_____

_____

_____

口說能力測驗

🔊 Track 69

請在 15 秒內完成並唸出下列自我介紹的句子：

My seat number is （座位號碼後 5 碼）, and my test number is （考試號碼後 5 碼）.

第一部分：複誦 🔊 Track 70

共五題，經由音檔播出，每題播出兩次，兩次之間約有一至二秒的間隔。聽完兩次後，請立即複誦一次。

第二部分：朗讀句子與短文 🔊 Track 71

共有五個句子及一篇短文，請先利用一分鐘的時間閱讀句子與短文，然後在一分鐘內以正常的速度，清楚正確地朗讀一遍，閱讀時請不要發出聲音。

One:　　Please contact Helen at 092–540–7936.

Two:　　It was difficult for me to make friends.

Three:　They have a collection of paintings there.

Four:　One of the things I miss most is the food.

Five:　It's not as heavy as I expected.

Six:　To get good grades in the exam, I decided to make a study plan. First, I'll read every chapter before class. Second, I'll pay more attention to what the teacher says. Third, I'll take notes during class. Notes are helpful to me when I review books.

第三部分：回答問題 🔊 Track 72

共七題。經由音檔播出，每題播出兩次，兩次之間約有一至二秒的間隔。聽完兩次後，請立即回答，每題回答時間 15 秒，請在作答時間內盡量地表達。

請將下列自我介紹的句子再唸一遍：

My seat number is （座位號碼後 5 碼）, and my test number is （考試號碼後 5 碼）.

全民英檢初級模擬試題
TEST 10

聽力測驗
第一部分　看圖辨義
第二部分　問答
第三部分　簡短對話
第四部分　短文聽解

閱讀能力測驗
第一部分　詞彙
第二部分　段落填空
第三部分　閱讀理解

寫作能力測驗
第一部分　單句寫作
第二部分　段落寫作

口說能力測驗
第一部分　複誦
第二部分　朗讀句子與短文
第三部分　回答問題

聽力測驗 | 本測驗分四個部分，皆為單選題，共 30 題，作答時間約 20 分鐘。作答說明為中文，印在試題冊上並由音檔播出。

第一部分：看圖辨義 🔊 Track 73

共 5 題，每題請聽音檔播出題目和三個英語句子之後，選出與所看到的圖畫最相符的答案。每題只播出一遍。

A. Question 1

Answer ❶：＿＿＿＿＿

B. Question 2

Answer ❷：＿＿＿＿＿

C. Question 3

Answer ❸ : _____

D. Questions 4 and 5

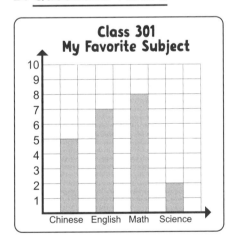

Answer ❹ : _____   ❺ : _____

第二部分：問答 🔊 Track 74

共 10 題，每題請聽音檔播出的英語句子，再從試題冊上三個回答中，選出一個最適合的答案。每題只播出一遍。

❻ _____
A. It's a deal.
B. None of your business.
C. Not at all.

❼ _____
A. I don't need a book. I need a room.
B. Could you please take my order now?
C. That's too bad. Are there any other hotels around here?

❽ _____
A. Yes, I work in the hospital.
B. Yes, I'm out of work.
C. I'm busy all the time.

❾ _____
A. No, that's your question.
B. No, I can't think of anything.
C. If you ask me, I'll say no way.

❿ _____
A. I'm sorry. The flight was called off.
B. I will try, but it might be tomorrow morning.
C. Sure. I will delete those files for you.

⓫ _____
A. Yes, it's quite cold outside.
B. Yes, I love to watch fashion shows.
C. Yes, I'd love to get out before it gets too dark.

⓬ _____
A. Take your time. There is no rush.
B. Hey, don't push me.
C. They are talking about you behind your back.

⓭ _____
A. How interesting!
B. For about seven days.
C. That sounds terrible!

⓮ _____
A. Oh, I don't think you are silly.
B. Really? What happened?
C. I can understand that.

⓯ _____
A. Pay with a credit card or cash?
B. The fitting room is over there.
C. Of course. What size are you?

第三部分：簡短對話 🔊 Track 75

共 10 題，每題請聽音檔播出一段對話和一個相關的問題後，再從試題冊上三個選項中，選出一個最適合的答案。每段對話和問題播出一遍。

⑯ _____
A. His neighbor is noisy.
B. The house is small.
C. It takes him a long time to get to work.

⑰ _____
A. Go to the mountains.
B. Take a road trip.
C. Go to a lake.

⑱ _____
A. A novel.
B. A movie.
C. A magazine.

⑲ _____
A. She ran twenty one meters today.
B. She ran twelve hours today.
C. She won the half marathon today.

⑳ _____
A. Ten.
B. Thirteen.
C. Thirty.

㉑ _____
A. A double cheeseburger.
B. A bacon cheeseburger.
C. A double bacon burger.

㉒ _____
A. Chocolate.
B. Clothes.
C. Flowers.

㉓ _____
A. Neither the man nor the woman has been to Orchid Island.
B. The woman has much money.
C. The man doesn't like to go to Orchid Island.

㉔ _____
A. At a brunch restaurant.
B. At a barbershop.
C. At a grocery.

㉕ _____
A. To a park.
B. To a church.
C. To a post office.

TEST **10** Listening

第四部分：短文聽解 🔊 Track 76

共 5 題，每題有三個圖片選項。請聽音檔播出的題目，並選出一個最適合的圖片。每題播出一遍。

㉖ _____

A.  B. 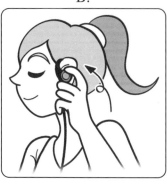 C.

㉗ _____

A.  B.  C.

㉘ _____

A.  B.  C.

㉙ _____

A.

B.

C.

㉚ _____

A.

B.

C.

閱讀能力測驗 ▌本測驗分三部分，全部都是單選題，共 30 題，作答時間 35 分鐘。

第一部分：詞彙

共 10 題，每個題目裡有一個空格。請從四個選項中選出一個最適合題意的字或詞作答。

_____ ❶ You're really _____. Could you please keep quiet for a while?

    A. sweet   B. effective   C. unique   D. talkative

_____ ❷ In the past, people put _____ on meat to keep it for a long time.

    A. roses   B. salt   C. cheese   D. metal

_____ ❸ Let's _____ and enjoy the dessert in the park!

    A. go on vacation   B. go on a picnic   C. go on a trip   D. go on a diet

_____ ❹ The more properly you eat, the _____ you will be.

    A. hotter   B. heavier   C. higher   D. healthier

_____ ❺ To get good _____, you have to review the book every day.

    A. groups   B. grapes   C. grades   D. guides

_____ ❻ Each student has to stand in front of the class _____ and make a self-introduction.

    A. in case   B. in panic   C. in turn   D. in tune

_____ ❼ Don't worry. I will finish my work in a _____ and hand it in on time.

    A. mood   B. word   C. moment   D. row

_____ ❽ The _____ from Taipei to Singapore takes about four hours.

    A. flight   B. distance   C. rate   D. weight

_____ ❾ Linda is always there when I need to cry on someone's _____.

    A. chest   B. back   C. stomach   D. shoulder

_____ ❿ The sailors felt lucky to have _____ the deadly storm.

    A. lived up to   B. lived through   C. passed away   D. passed by

第二部分：段落填空

共 8 題，包括二個段落，每個段落各含四個空格。每格均有四個選項，請依文意選出最適合的答案。

Questions 11–14

Playing basketball is my favorite   (11)   . I invited some of my classmates and friends to join me. We   (12)   a team at the beginning of the semester and practiced together after school. We all enjoyed the feeling of shooting the ball into the net. Besides   (13)   alone, we sometimes played games with students from other classes. Of course, we won most of the time.   (14)   , more and more classmates joined our team. I believe we will become the strongest team in school in the future, even stronger than our school team.

⑪ _____
A. subject
B. place
C. event
D. sport

⑬ _____
A. to practice
B. practice
C. practiced
D. practicing

⑫ _____
A. formed
B. shaped
C. turned
D. set

⑭ _____
A. Without your support
B. As we lose the game
C. Inspired by our spirit
D. Divided into different team

Questions 15–18

Do you sometimes forget to tell your mother that you love her? Do you sometimes forget to thank your mother for all the wonderful things   (15)   ? Many people forget to do that which is why in many countries there is a national holiday to   (16)   everyone to appreciate their mothers. People everywhere try to make their mothers feel special on this day   (17)   buying them flowers, writing poems, making cards, serving them breakfast in bed, or doing all the chores around the house for the day to give their mothers a rest.

Mother's day is a good day to make your mother feel special, but you don't have to wait until that day   (18)   . Every day is a chance to do something nice for her. So just do it now without delay.

⑮ _____

A. she has never done before

B. she has done for you

C. you have done for your mother

D. that never happened

⑯ _____

A. judge

B. inform

C. remind

D. hint

⑰ _____

A. by

B. in

C. about

D. of

⑱ _____

A. has arrived

B. arrived

C. arrive

D. arrives

第三部分：閱讀理解

共 12 題，包括 4 個題組，每個題組含 1 至 2 篇短文，與數個相關的四選一的選擇題。請由試題冊上的選項中選出最適合的答案。

Questions 19–21

YOU CAN NOW SHOP ONLINE!

BIGshop is one of Australia's fastest growing online department stores. Shop here using our safe universal shopping cart technology for thousands of products.

SHOP NOW >

_____ ⑲ Why would a person check out its website?

A. To get the movie tickets

B. To buy products on the Internet

C. To join a club

D. To watch a video

⑳ Where is the BIGshop located?

A. In Austria

B. In America

C. In Australia

D. At shoppers' home

㉑ How many types of products are there at BIGshop?

A. Several thousands

B. Several hundreds

C. Several hundred thousands

D. Several thousand hundreds

Questions 22–24

Easy Salad for You to Make at Home

Ingredients:

- 4 - 6 tomatoes
- 1 cucumber
- 1 green pepper
- 1 red onion
- 2 tablespoons olive oil
- A few leaves of mint
- Small pinch of salt
- Thick slice of feta cheese

Instructions:

1. Wash the tomatoes, cucumber, green pepper and red onion then dice them.
2. Combine the four ingredients in a bowl.
3. Drizzle in the olive oil and sparkle with the salt and mint leaves.
4. Cut the cheese into cubes and sprinkle them on top.
5. Serve with crusty bread and enjoy!

Total preparation time: 20 minutes.

Servings: 6

_____ ㉒ What is this article mainly about?

    A. To teach people how to make an easy salad

    B. To cook delicious food for your family

    C. To add lemon flavor to the salad

    D. To teach people how to buy fruit

_____ ㉓ According to the recipe, how many servings does it make?

    A. One

    B. Eight

    C. Six

    D. Twenty

_____ ㉔ According to the recipe, which of the following statements is **NOT** true?

    A. It takes you 20 minutes to make this salad.

    B. Crusty bread should be prepared.

    C. The first step is to clean some ingredients.

    D. Don't forget to bake the salad in the oven for 5 minutes.

Questions 25–27

_____ ㉕ If you want to attend this party, what should you do first?

    A. The information is not provided on this invitation.

    B. Call Adel and let her know that you will go to the party.

    C. Call Peggy at 222-836-659 and tell her you will be there.

    D. Send a letter to Peggy's parents and tell them that you are happy for Peggy.

❷❻ Which may be the birthday cake for Peggy?

A.

B.

C.

D.

_____ ❷❼ What should Peggy's friends wear to the party?

A. Sport coat

B. Swimsuit

C. Clothing that people wear in bed

D. Clothing that people wear on formal occasions

Questions 28–30

People can find everything they want to know on the Internet as long as they click the search button. Indeed, Google is a popular choice for web search engine. Its name originally came from the word googol, a math related term. Currently, over 90 percent of people around the world find information on Google. Therefore, "google" was added to English dictionaries. That means searching for something on the Internet. In 1996, this great web search engine was created by Larry Page and Sergey Brin. Because of being willing to have new ideas and break with tradition, "google.com" was soon a success in the following years. People who work there have difficult but interesting work to do. That's why many useful and popular services and products have been made.

_____ ❷❽ What is this article mainly about?

A. The owner of Google

B. The introduction of Google

C. The method of doing a search on Google

D. The way Google hires people

_____ ㉙ From this article, what was the main reason that made Google successful?

    A. It was good at putting advertisements online.

    B. It was able to make changes.

    C. It had the most advanced computers.

    D. Its name was added to dictionaries.

_____ ㉚ What information about Google is **NOT** provided in this article?

    A. The number of its workers

    B. The names of its creators

    C. The origin of its name

    D. The reason for its success

寫作能力測驗 ▋

第一部分：單句寫作

　　　　請將答案寫在答案欄中，如有文法、用字、拼字、標點符號、大小寫等錯誤，將予扣分。

第 1～5 題：句子改寫

　　請依題目之提示，將原句改寫成指定型式，並將改寫的句子**完整**地寫在答案欄中。*注意：每題均需寫出完整的句子，否則將予扣分。*

① Is that a good tooth?（改複數句）

_____?

② Paul gave me a lot of toys.

I _____.

③ Henry: Would you like to go out with me?

Lily: Yes, I'd love to.

Lily was willing to _____.

④ To say rude words is not polite.

It is _____.

⑤ We had fun playing volleyball on the beach.（改為 had a good time）

_____.

第 6～10 題：句子合併

　　請依照題目指示，將兩句合併成一句，並將合併的句子**完整**地寫在答案欄中。*注意：每題均需寫出完整的句子，否則將予扣分。*

⑥ Albert jogs every morning.

Albert has gotten used to it.

_____.

⑦ Sophia is not honest.

I'm telling the truth.（用 To tell... 合併）

_____.

❽ My brother is a college student now.

My brother went to college three years ago.（用 for 合併）

_____ .

❾ Martha is reading a novel.

The novel is about a hero in the 16th century.（用 about 合併）

_____ .

❿ I know a man.

The man's dog is from Germany.（用 whose 合併）

_____ .

第 11～15 題：重組

請將題目中所有提示字詞整合成一有意義的句子，並將重組的句子**完整**地寫在答案欄中。**注意：每題均需寫出完整的句子。答案中必須使用所有提示字詞，且不能隨意增減字詞及標點符號，否則不予計分。**

⓫ These _____ .

air cleaners / plants / act / as / can

⓬ God _____ .

themselves / who / those / help / helps

⓭ You _____ .

cheat / not / had / on the exams / better

⓮ The heavy rain _____ .

food / prices / the rise / caused / in

⓯ He _____ .

his wife / smoking/ was giving / quit / because / birth

第二部分：段落寫作

題目：請根據以下圖片寫一篇約 50 字的短文，描寫你所遭遇的事件。*注意：未依提示作答者，將予扣分。*

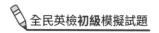

口說能力測驗

🔊 Track 77

請在 15 秒內完成並唸出下列自我介紹的句子：

My seat number is （座位號碼後 5 碼）, and my test number is （考試號碼後 5 碼）.

第一部分：複誦 🔊 Track 78

共五題，經由音檔播出，每題播出兩次，兩次之間約有一至二秒的間隔。聽完兩次後，請立即複誦一次。

第二部分：朗讀句子與短文 🔊 Track 79

共有五個句子及一篇短文，請先利用一分鐘的時間閱讀句子與短文，然後在一分鐘內以正常的速度，清楚正確地朗讀一遍，閱讀時請不要發出聲音。

One: I would have passed the exam if I'd studied harder.

Two: Doesn't it get you angry when people cut in line?

Three: Would you mind giving me an extra blanket?

Four: You have a better job and a bigger car than me.

Five: Room 1218 is a non-smoking room.

Six: Technology has changed many things in my life. For example, when I was a student, I used to take a bus to school. Now I take the MRT or drive my car to my office. Besides, I can carry the notebook computer with me and use the Internet everywhere.

第三部分：回答問題 🔊 Track 80

共七題。經由音檔播出，每題播出兩次，兩次之間約有一至二秒的間隔。聽完兩次後，請立即回答，每題回答時間 15 秒，請在作答時間內盡量地表達。

請將下列自我介紹的句子再唸一遍：

My seat number is （座位號碼後 5 碼）, and my test number is （考試號碼後 5 碼）.

全民英檢聽力測驗 SO EASY (中級篇)

三民英語編輯小組 彙整

◆ 完全符合新制全民英檢中級聽力測驗,讓你掌握最新題型。

◆ 全書共 8 回,情境、用字、語法等皆符合全民英檢中級程度。

◆ 提供試題範例分析,精闢解說各題型解題技巧與出題方向。

◆ 解析採用活動式的夾冊設計,讓你輕鬆對照題目,方便閱讀。

◆ 隨書附電子朗讀音檔,由專業外籍錄音員錄製。讓你培養語感、提升應試熟悉度。

全民英檢中級模擬試題 (修訂三版)

符合全民英檢最新題型

讓你輕鬆應試!

★ **聽說讀寫樣樣都有**
一次完整收錄初、複試的試題,共 6 回模擬試題,輕鬆熟悉全民英檢中級所有考題。

★ **全真模擬測驗模式**
版面仿照英檢測驗,融入核心素養,情境、用字、文章皆符合全民英檢中級程度。

★ **附電子朗讀音檔**
由專業外籍錄音員錄製,讓你提升應試熟悉度。

★ **附解析附冊**
方便完整對照中英題目及選項,有效理解考題脈絡。

郭慧敏 編著

國家圖書館出版品預行編目資料

全民英檢初級模擬試題／Barbara Kuo編著.——修訂
四版二刷.——臺北市：三民，2023
　　面；　公分

　ISBN 978-957-14-7335-2　（平裝）
　1. 英語 2. 讀本

805.1892　　　　　　　　　　　110018293

全民英檢初級模擬試題

編 著 者	Barbara Kuo
內頁繪圖	豆 子
發 行 人	劉振強
出 版 者	三民書局股份有限公司
地　　址	臺北市復興北路 386 號 (復北門市) 臺北市重慶南路一段 61 號 (重南門市)
電　　話	(02)25006600
網　　址	三民網路書店 https://www.sanmin.com.tw
出版日期	初版一刷 2008 年 8 月 修訂四版一刷 2022 年 3 月 修訂四版二刷 2023 年 10 月
書籍編號	S807270
I S B N	978-957-14-7335-2

三民書局